STARLIGHT HOLLOW

STARLIGHT HOLLOW
BOOK 1

YASMINE GALENORN

A Nightqueen Enterprises LLC Publication

Published by Yasmine Galenorn

PO Box 2037, Kirkland WA 98083-2037

STARLIGHT HOLLOW

A Starlight Hollow Novel

Copyright © 2023 by Yasmine Galenorn

First Electronic Printing: 2023 Nightqueen Enterprises LLC

First Print Edition: 2023 Nightqueen Enterprises

Cover Art & Design: Ravven

Art Copyright: Yasmine Galenorn

Editor: Elizabeth Flynn

A Nightqueen Enterprises LLC Publication

Published in the United States of America

ACKNOWLEDGMENTS

Welcome to the world of Starlight Hollow.

Thanks to my usual crew: Samwise, my husband, Andria and Jennifer—without their help, I'd be swamped. To the women who have helped me find my way in indie, you're all great, and thank you to everyone. To my wonderful cover artist, Ravven, for the beautiful work she's done, and to my editor, Elizabeth, who helps me keep my ellipses under control—thank you both.

Also, my love to my furbles, who keep me happy. My most reverent devotion to Mielikki, Tapio, Ukko, Rauni, and Brighid, my spiritual guardians and guides. My love and reverence to Herne, and Cernunnos, and to the Fae, who still rule the wild places of this world. And a nod to the Wild Hunt, which runs deep in my magick, as well as in my fiction.

You can find me through my website at **Galenorn.com** and be sure to sign up for my **newsletter** to keep updated on all my latest releases! You can find my advice on writing, discussions about the books, and general ramblings on my **YouTube channel**. If you liked this book, I'd be grateful if you'd leave a review—it helps more than you can think.

November 2023
Brightest Blessings,
~The Painted Panther~
~Yasmine Galenorn~

WELCOME TO STARLIGHT HOLLOW

Welcome to Starlight Hollow, a small town on Hood Canal,
Washington, where dreams become nightmares, and nightmares
become reality.

My name is Elphyra MacPherson, and I was born into a
lineage of witches from thousands of years back. The women
of my family have always lived between the worlds, our blood
as full of magic as our souls are. Born from Scottish descent,
we guard over towns and villages. We're found in cities and
the country, and each of us is charged with keeping the
monsters and the storms at bay—using any means needed.

After tragedy invades my life, I move to Starlight Hollow,
a little town near Gig Harbor, where I find new friends and
Fancypants—a dragonette. Together with him and my circle
of friends, I muddle through life, love, and danger, as best as
I can.

But when I'm approached by Darla, a woman who's
dealing with a demonic presence haunting her house, my life
begins to change. Not only am I facing danger from the spirit
world, but I also face another challenge when Faron

Collinsworth, the King of the Olympic Wolf Pack, approaches me.

We've already had two bad encounters, but now he wants my help. Members of the community are being murdered and the sheriff thinks one of the Wolf King's Pack is to blame. Even as I try to eradicate the demons at the hell house, Faron asks me to exonerate his lieutenant. But that may not be possible, and as the killer digs deep, I must focus on what I'm able to do, as opposed to what I wish I could do.

But will Faron and I find out the truth before we end up killing each other?

CHAPTER ONE

AFTER STOPPING AT THE POST OFFICE AND HEADING downtown, I swung into a parking spot directly in front of my friend's shop and hopped out of my car—a midnight blue Chevy Equinox. I frowned at the sun, grateful for my sunglasses.

I didn't like heat. I didn't like the *sun*—the heat and light had an angry feel, and fire elementals were almost always destructive. It was their nature, of course, but that didn't make them any less dangerous. Thanks to climate change, they were becoming more active, so we were going to have to get used to dealing with them.

In addition to spring, summer, autumn, and winter, we now had a fifth season—wildfire season, during which the smoke blanketed the sky. Luckily, smoke season wasn't as predictable as Mama Nature's normal four, but each year it grew worse.

At least here in western Washington, summers weren't horrible, but I still missed the rain. Granted, it *was* June—technically, the time for sun—but that didn't mean I had to like it. I came alive during the dark, gloomy days of autumn and winter.

I strode across the sidewalk in two steps, hopping over a crack, to push open the door to the Olympic Forest Expeditions Company. I wasn't in the market for a guide through the Olympics, but thanks to the letter in my hand, I needed the advice of my best friend, Bree Loomis.

Unfortunately, she was busy with a group of tourists. I stood to one side, frustrated, hoping she would notice me. Which she did. She was a puma shifter with a laser focus that expanded to include everything within eyeshot. She held up her hand, sidling away from the clients who were peppering her with questions.

"One second, please," she said. "I'll only be a moment."

Bree headed over to join me. She was dressed for the job —jeans, a flannel shirt neatly tucked in, and hiking boots. At five-nine, Bree was four inches taller than I was, but I was curvier with an hourglass figure. We were both muscled, though her muscle was more obvious while mine was padded with boobs and hips. Her mid-shoulder blond hair was swept back in a tidy French braid. I wore my waist-length flame-red hair in a mass of waves wilder than the ocean.

"Looking good," she said, glancing over my outfit. "Special occasion?"

I snorted. "When do I *ever* have a special occasion? You know I'm a leather fiend," I said. I was wearing a pair of leather jeans that laced up the sides, exposing a two-inch strip of skin on either side, a black cotton halter top, knee-high black platform boots, and opera-length fingerless gloves. "Can you take a break? I need coffee and I need to talk about *this*." I held up a letter, grimacing. The contents had left me shaken.

Bree glanced at the letter. "You *always* need coffee. Sorry. Remember, I *own* this joint? I don't get breaks," she said.

"Can you wait till five?" She glanced at the clock. "It's three-thirty now."

I sighed. I was impatient, but I was also aware that I made my own hours. Hers were printed on the sign on the door. "I'll be back in ninety minutes. Dinner?"

"That I can do. See you at five." She winked at me and returned to her clients.

They looked both excited and scared, and I wondered where she was going to take them. Half the clients Bree catered to were top-of-the-line fit, ready to go ziplining through the forests or descending into abandoned mine shafts. The other half looked like they could barely manage riding inner tubes down a low-flowing stream. Both sets usually came away happy and satisfied.

I headed back into the streets.

I'd lived in Starlight Hollow for nearly six months, and it had become home in a short time. The town was quirky, and it lived nestled in shadow. The populace had the requisite artists and writers, inventors and oddballs who all found the Olympic Peninsula a comfortable haven, but beneath the veneer, there were also some lost souls who lived here. Old hippies who had tripped one too many times and lived on the edge of reality made their homes here, along with the occasional survivalists holed up waiting for Ragnarok or Armageddon. The survivalists tended to bury themselves up in the foothills of the Olympics rather than in the town proper, thankfully.

A couple communes established their footprints in the surrounding hills, and I was pretty certain a cult or two had decided this was *the* place to be. In addition, several shifter organizations were headquartered here, and of course we drew in the requisite ghost hunters and paranormal investigators, because Starlight Hollow was the most haunted town in the state.

An invisible shadow hovered over the town, created by the ghosts of the past, the creatures who hid in the woods, and the souls who were dead, and those living who didn't want to be found. But most of the residents were pleasant enough. Founded in 1855 by Scottish immigrants, the original settlers had brought their own spirits and legends with them and a unique culture had evolved. One that had its wonderful side, yet specters lurked in the thickets of one of the four rainforests of the United States. And around here, the earth and water elementals were strong, and the months of rain and fog and drizzle empowered me.

With a population of around three thousand, Starlight Hollow didn't exactly invite tourism, and the unofficial town slogan wasn't open-armed. Nothing said "Welcome to our town" like: *Starlight Hollow: Where dreams become nightmares, and nightmares become reality.* But for those who felt invited in by the town, life *could* remain a dream.

I didn't care about ghosts or monsters—I could handle most of them, though my real strength was in the forest and lakes, the earth and the sea. I'd been trained since birth to cope with the paranormal. Hell, I *was* paranormal incarnate. As for the storms, I welcomed them, drawing my power from them, and when the winds raged I would weave my charms to try and appease the gods of air. Yes, I could handle most things...except vampires. I *hated* vampires, and wanted nothing to do with any of them. Of course, there was no guarantee that Starlight Hollow was vamp-free, but none had been spotted or mentioned, and that was good enough for me.

So I had ninety minutes to kill. I didn't want to go grocery shopping because I didn't want to leave frozen food in the car for that long, so I decided to head for the plant nursery. I needed more primroses and johnny jump-ups for the walkway, and they could survive in the car for a few hours until I arrived home. I tucked the letter away, not wanting to think about it until I could talk to Bree. She always helped me get my head on straight.

I drove down by the edge of the bay to The Grapevine—a plant nursery. The parking lot—and the town—was located right on the edge of Dabob Bay. The store was huge, bigger than the grocery stores around town. Not a surprise, given the number of small farmers who lived in the area.

As I pushed through the double doors, the smell of flowers and plants overwhelmed me and I smiled. The store smelled of life—plants and soil and all the wonderful things that belonged to the earth. And the earth was my source of power, and her woodlands and waters, my sanctuary.

"Elphyra! Back so soon?" Tracy, the owner, saw me and hurried over. "Are the flowers all right? Did they die?"

I laughed. "No worries. No, they're doing great, at least so far. We'll see how long I can keep them alive. I need more, though, to finish the walkway. Probably about half of what I bought last time."

I found a handcart—large enough to handle bags of fertilizer as well as plants—and threaded my way through the aisles until I was facing a series of shelves filled with flowers. I preferred primroses, given they were perennials, and I sorted through them, looking for the right colors. I wanted my walkway lined in purple and fuchsia and crimson. I could feel the plants. They sensed my intent, and there was a quiet excitement.

There was no way to explain it—plants didn't "think" like people, they didn't have the same kind of sentience that people and animals did, but there was a basic understanding of the difference between life and death. And when you went further out—onto the astral plane—you could find the great Devas, the oversouls of each plant type, which were like what you might call a hive mind. All of the blackberry bushes in the world were part of the great

Blackberry Deva, for instance, which was greater than the sum of its parts.

After I found enough flowers to finish the walkway, I added ferns. My property overflowed with ferns, but I didn't want to bother with cuttings or digging up existing ones and moving them. I added an array of fiddlehead ferns, maidenhair ferns, western sword ferns, deer ferns, and lady ferns. On my way to the cashier, I added several packages of wildflower seeds and a few six-packs of marigolds.

"Buying out the store?" Tracy asked, coming around to my side with the barcode scanner. "It's easier if I do this than have you move everything up to the register," she added. "So, how are you enjoying life in Starlight Hollow?"

Much like New Englanders, the folks of Starlight Hollow saw everybody who had moved to town during the past decade as a newcomer, though I'd grown up in Port Townsend, a mere forty-five minutes away. I wasn't a local here. At least, not yet.

I leaned against the counter. "So far, so good. I've been here almost six months now, and I feel like I'm really starting to settle in. I've been mulling over what I want to do with the land." I had three acres. "I'm going to be building raised beds for my herb garden next, I think. I should get them in before the autumn comes, so the plants have time to acclimate."

"How's the cottage?" Tracy asked, shooting me a sideways look. "Mrs. Jansen was always so particular about her home."

"Oh, it's fine. I think she's gone—I don't sense her there. I have the workshop where I'll eventually be meeting clients, selling spell components and home-grown herb mixtures and so forth." I caught one of the flower containers that almost fell off the cart, pushing it back on.

"I'd love to see the cottage now that you own it," she said. "Mrs. Jansen always had it decked out in Scandinavian décor. Do you have any Scandinavian in you?"

Though the question felt personal, I realized she was curious. "Probably, back along the line. My mother's Scottish, but family stories say that back in the Middle Ages her people married into the line of Viking invaders. So my mother's Scottish and Norse. Her family came to the States in the 1800s. On my father's side, though, I'm pretty much all Scottish. His father and mother were immigrants."

"Interesting," Tracy said. "I'm fourth-generation Italian." She finished ringing up the flowers and started in on the ferns. "So, you think old lady Jansen crossed over? I always wondered. She loved that house."

"I haven't seen hide nor hair of her—the cottage felt cleansed when I first walked into it. I understand why she loved it, though. I've come to love the place, too. It's perfect —and then I also have the workshop that's fully heated, and I also have plenty of storage space in the utility shed. Along with the acreage, I can build my own world." I could tell she was angling for an invitation to come out and snoop around, but delicately avoided offering her the chance. Tracy was nice, but she was definitely the town gossip and she had a mouth on her a mile wide and as loud as an air raid siren.

"Well, I'm glad you settled in with us," she said, returning to the cash register. "That will be one hundred thirty-five dollars and twenty-eight cents."

I handed her my credit card and she rang it through. "Here you go, and here's your receipt. Maybe I'll schedule a reading with you sometime and come out to take a look around," she added, handing me back my card.

I tucked it back in my wallet and slung my purse over my shoulder. "You know where to find me." I smiled, hoping she'd never act on the thought. "Thanks for the flowers! They're beautiful."

"Do you want some help loading them into your car?" she called as I pushed the cart toward the door.

"No, I'm good. Thanks anyway."

As I left the store and pushed the cart over to my car, I pressed the button on my key fob to unlock the liftgate of my SUV. It opened as I trundled the cart over and loaded the flowers into the back, onto a tarp. I had barely finished when the wind picked up, washing the smell of brine and seaweed across me. Nothing said home to me more than that smell— brine and seaweed and the sharp scent of saltwater.

Dabob Bay was an internal bay connected to Hood Canal, which was actually a saltwater fjord. The Navy had its claws deep into the area, given there was a naval base in Bremerton as well as the Bangor Trident Submarine Base, headquartered on the other side of the bay. Civilians enjoyed the estuary as well, and during open seasons, locals went fishing and crabbing in the water. Conservancy groups had worked with the Navy, throwing money into maintaining the ecology of the bay and protecting it from overdevelopment. And several groups, from Selkies to witches aligned with the water elementals, played liaison to ensure that nothing went awry on the magical end.

I glanced at my phone. It was four-fifteen. After returning the cart to the nursery, I wandered over to the winding wooden staircase that led to the narrow beach next to the water. A concrete ramp next to the steps provided handicapped access.

The water called to me, and I was pretty sure I could hear one of the local Selkies singing. Their voices echoed through the water but, unlike the sirens, they didn't lure people in. Their songs were comforting, if mournful. I followed the stairs down to the beach.

Cautious—the beach was rocky, primarily made up of pebbles covering the sand and soil—I followed the shore to a nearby driftwood log. It was near the beginning of the beach, but I could still see the high-water marks that had covered the shoreline, a few feet closer to the bay. As I sat on the log, the tide rippled, the waves rolling in but then washing out farther with each cycle. A reader board near the bottom of the stairs predicted low tide in about two and a half hours.

I closed my eyes and drew in the energy. It flooded my senses, spreading through me in ripples, calming me as it washed past. There was an immensity about the water, even fjords, lakes, and ponds. The oceans and seas were massive, threatening to swamp and overwhelm, but the smaller bodies of water had their own feel. And our bodies responded, if we only listened, given we were close to ninety percent water ourselves.

I was warm in my leather. It was sixty-eight degrees. But most of the year round, Starlight Hollow—and the Quilcene area—received far more precipitation than farther up the peninsula. In fact, the town received almost *fifty-five inches* of rain annually. Dabob Bay was good for swimming, although no matter where you were in the Pacific Northwest, if there were tides, you always had to watch for rip currents.

As I sat there, meditating, my phone rang. I glanced at it. My mother, *again*. I'd let her last two calls go to voicemail. I loved her, but I was a disappointment to her in many ways and I didn't want to hear yet again about how I had failed the family. I contemplated not answering, but she was as stubborn as me. I bit the bullet and hit the speakerphone.

"Hey," I said.

"Hey? That's all you have to say? Are you all right? I've called twice—"

"I'm fine. I've just been busy." I cut her off. I wasn't in a mood to bicker. "What's up? What do you need?"

There was a silence on the other end of the line for a moment, then she said, "I wanted to make sure you were okay. When I don't hear from you for a while, I worry."

I sighed. Given everything that had happened, she had a

right to worry and I couldn't refute that. "I'm okay. I've been planting flowers and getting my workshop ready. I want to walk every inch of the acreage and create a few access trails through the undergrowth."

Another pause, and my mother said, "Well, that sounds nice. I'd love to see your new home." And there we were. She wanted to come visit.

"Once I have everything set, I'll invite you and Aunt Ciara and Owen down to visit. I promise." I tried to work some enthusiasm into my voice.

"I'd like that. We all would. I want you to be happy again, Elphyra. That's all I have ever wanted—for you to be happy."

Feeling suddenly guilty for my snippy attitude, I let out a sigh. "I know, Mom. I know you want the best for me."

She hesitated, then said, "I dreamed I was walking out in a forest and I came to a stream. I saw the Washing Woman, Elphyra. She was washing a bloody sheet." Her voice fell and she let out a soft cry.

I caught my breath. "No...did she speak?"

The Washing Woman—or the Washer at the Ford—was one of the bean nighe, a death spirit. There were several of them and one had been attached to my father's clan for centuries. She could appear in dreams, as well as in the flesh. And it was always when someone in the clan was about to die.

"Did she tell you who's been marked?" Even as I said it, I knew the answer. The Washer never gave names unless it was the person who saw her, and then she would point to them.

My mother was always the one the Washer came to—at least she was since she had married my father. The Washer chose who she visited carefully, and my mother had been singled out. But then again, her family and my father's family were from the same general area, and they were members of the same clan, so it wasn't surprising.

"No. And you know the Washer usually doesn't appear when the death is natural."

I almost told her about the letter I'd received from my great-grandmother—my father's grandmother—but I decided to wait. I needed time to think. "Well, tell Ciara and Owen to be careful."

"I will. But please, anything can happen—you know that better than anybody. Be careful, darling. When the bean nighe appears, she can summon anyone."

"Don't worry about me, please. I like it here, and I think —in time—I'll be happy again. I need time to process everything, and I couldn't do it if I was back there. I'm good—I may not be happy, but I'm content."

"Well, then, I guess I'll let you get back to your planting. Call me in a few days?"

"I promise," I said. "I'll talk to you soon."

And with that, I hung up and went back to watching the water.

CHAPTER TWO

A SPEEDBOAT CIRCLED THE BAY NEAR THE OPPOSITE SHORE. Nearly forty miles long and over one and a half miles wide, Dabob Bay was also a tidal wetlands system, still in the process of being restored to a pristine condition with invasive and non-endemic species slowly being weeded out.

I glanced at my phone. It was four forty-five, time to head back to Bree's shop. I retraced my steps to the stairs and the parking lot. Along the way, I mulled over the phone call.

At least I had told my mother the truth. Moving to Starlight Hollow *had* been good for me, so far. I still had post-traumatic stress disorder, but getting away from Port Townsend had helped. Though Port Townsend was forty-five minutes up the coastline, the mood of Starlight Hollow seemed a million miles away.

The wind had become gusty as I parked in a shady spot in front of Bree's shop and slipped out of the car. She was sitting at her desk, alone, as I pushed through the front door.

"Back on time," I said.

"Give me five and I'll be ready to go," Bree said. "Where do you want to eat?"

I grinned. "Where do you think?" While I liked a number of different cuisines, my favorite always came back to one restaurant.

She rolled her eyes. "All right, fine. Roland's Steakhouse again. At least they have a variety."

"They make the best clam chowder around. And fried shrimp," I added.

"I love you, but I have to tell you—you have the appetite of a trucker from the Midwest. Meat and potatoes. Are you sure you don't want to try something different?" Bree slipped her backpack over her shoulder. "I'm ready."

I waited as she set the alarm and locked the door. "I may not be adventurous with food, but sometimes basic is a good thing."

We split up, taking our separate cars to the steakhouse, which was on the south side of town—nearer my home. Bree lived on the north side.

Roland's Steakhouse was rustic, but their food was fantastic. Roland had never met a steak he couldn't grill. I leaned against my car, waiting for Bree, and she pulled in a couple minutes after I had. We went in the restaurant together and were seated within five minutes. The restaurant's busy time was during lunch, and after six.

"I'll have a café mocha," I said. I didn't want to drink since I was driving. In fact, I seldom drank more than a few sips anymore.

"Coffee for me. Cream, no sugar." Bree leaned back in the booth and let out a sigh. "Business has picked up. I think I'm in for a busy summer. I may have to hire a part-time receptionist. I booked four trips today—and last week, I booked twelve. The calendar's filling up."

"How much does business fall during the off months?" I asked.

"Some, but there are always a few resilient folks who want

to hike Hurricane Ridge in the snow. I try to limit it to two trips a week, but I may have to open up another day." She paused, opening her menu. "So, how goes it?"

"My mother called today." I stared at my menu. "She saw the Washer Woman in a dream."

Bree took a breath. "Do you know who?"

I shook my head. "No, we don't. Not yet."

Bree and I had gone to the same high school together in Port Townsend. Then, she signed up for junior college to get her AA in business, while I attended a four-year college. We had been best friends then, and had stayed best friends, even after she moved to Starlight Hollow. She was one of the few who knew what I'd been through and she'd been there for me every step of the way.

"There's something else," Bree said. "I can hear it in your voice."

"You're not wrong there." I paused as the waitress brought our drinks and filled our water glasses.

"Would you like to order now?" she said.

I glanced at Bree, who nodded. "Yes, please. I want a twelve-ounce ribeye, medium rare, with extra butter, and add a lobster tail. Mashed potatoes and gravy, on the side. I'll have the fried calamari to start."

The waitress wrote my order down and turned to Bree. "And for you?"

"Lobster mac 'n cheese. A side salad with that, please. And to begin with, mozzarella sticks." Bree handed her menu to the waitress and waited until the woman walked away. "So, tell me what's up. Every time your mother calls, you want to go out to dinner or coffee."

I stirred my mocha. "Do I? Well, that shouldn't surprise me. I know she's worried about me—and gods know, she has reason to be. I fell apart after Rian died."

"That's putting it mildly," Bree said. "You shut down, girl.

You closed everything down and we were all worried you were going to kill yourself. I'm just being real about it."

I stared at my plate. "I did shut down. What the hell was I supposed to do?"

"Listen," Bree said. "Nobody else was there. Nobody can fully understand what horrors you went through. But in the aftermath, we had to sit on the sidelines and watch, and you didn't want us helping you to pick up the pieces. You might consider cutting your mom and aunt some slack."

After a long sip of my mocha, I finally caved. "All right. I get it—I know why she's checking up on me."

"She calls me, too, to check on you, you know." Bree rolled her eyes, but she didn't sound put out by it. "I tell her you're fine and busy."

"I didn't realize she was doing that." I wiped the foam off my lip. Maybe I was playing the hermit too much. My mother had been nothing but helpful during the crisis, and she had been there for me every step of the way while I was recovering. "Okay, I get it. I'll call her later and have a long talk to reassure her. But that's not why I asked you to dinner. Something else has come up and I need some advice."

The waitress appeared with our appetizers. Bree waited till she left. "What happened?"

I picked up my fork and stabbed one of the calamari, popping it in my mouth, then reached for my purse. "This came today. It's from my great-grandma. She lives on the island of Skye. My father's grandmother." I pulled the letter out of my purse and handed it to her.

She took it and began reading:

My great-granddaughter Elphyra:

Your mother told me what happened to you last year. She also told me that you have moved out and

15

bought a home. You should have come to me yourself
with the news. But whatever the case, I am coming to
stay with you for a while until I know that you're all
right. You don't heal up quickly from ordeals such as
you went through, but you're a MacPherson and of
strong stock. There are triggers in our family that can
skew your powers in the wrong direction. I'll be there in
a matter of weeks. There will be no discussion—this is
my word, and as the matriarch of the family clan, you
will welcome me into your home. Your great-gm,

Morgance

Bree glanced over the top of the page at me. "I hope your
guest room's ready."

"You don't think I can convince her to give up her plans?"
I knew the answer but needed to hear someone who knew my
family weigh in on it.

Bree snorted. "The only way you're going to get out of
this is to offer to fly over and stay with her, and somehow, I
don't think you're ready for that."

"No," I said. "I have no idea what she'll think of my
house. The cottage isn't that big, but at least I have a guest
room for her."

"Does she know you have tattoos?" Bree finished her
mozzarella sticks as the waitress showed up with our dinners.
She set the plates in front of us.

I sighed. "Can I get a lemonade?" The waitress nodded,
then headed toward the back. "No, she doesn't. I have no idea
what she'll think."

Both of my arms were covered—full sleeves of beautiful
tattoos that all wove together. A grotto, flowers, and fly
agaric, a tortie cat to commemorate the cat of my heart who
had been with me twelve years before she died. It had

happened all too suddenly and she died in my arms, with me cradling her, not understanding what was happening.

The vet performed a necropsy and found that she had succumbed to a rare kidney disease that presented when it was too late for treatment. Other images wove in—symbols representing Danu and the Dagda. A dragon. And a candle sitting on a skull with roses surrounding it—my newest one. That one had hurt bone-deep—and had left emotional scars. That tattoo was in memory of Rian, my late fiancé.

"What did you do today, beside mull over the letter?" Bree asked. She could always tell when my mood was spiraling.

I shrugged. "Planted flowers. And I bought some more—they're in the back of my car. I plan to finish the walkway tomorrow. Oh—I've been spending more time with my neighbor. May Anderson." I sighed as the sweet taste of lobster melted in my mouth. "This is good. The chef here knows his stuff, that's for sure."

"Yeah, the mac 'n cheese is the best I've tasted. You know, May's great. Everybody in town loves her. Well, almost everyone. She has a few enemies. Maybe 'rivals' is the right term. They envy her wins at the Starlight Hollow Autumn Fair." Bree grinned.

"Well, good luck to them changing that." I snorted, then sobered. "I like May. She has the most calming aura. Every time we've talked, I have felt at peace. And the basket was huge." Laughing, I described the massive welcome wagon gift I had received from May. "She filled it with homemade preserves, fruit, a honey-baked ham, fresh bread, a few magical oils that she makes, and a list of trusted handymen, gardeners, a plumber, and other service people whom she trusts."

"May's a fixture in Starlight Hollow. You can trust her." Bree tore open a biscuit and slathered it in butter, then offered me one.

"I feel like I can trust her. But...I have to tell you, the woods separating her land and mine make me nervous. I don't know why, but the trees feel...off." I shivered. "Maybe it's that I'm not used to living out on my own in the middle of nowhere. I don't know."

"I told you, Starlight Hollow's an odd place. You think Port Townsend has secrets? Starlight Hollow's secrets go deep, and there's no way to know when they started. But I still prefer living here to living in Port Townsend." Bree buttered a second roll.

"Are there any vampires around?" I asked.

Bree shrugged. "I don't think so. I haven't heard of any. This town may be odd, and there's a lot of dark history here, but vampires...I doubt they're welcome here. For one thing, Faron Collinsworth hates vampires and his Pack is headquartered here."

I grimaced. I hadn't met Faron, but he was a wolf shifter and that alone gave me the creeps. Most wolf shifters I knew, at least the men, were arrogant and patriarchal, a direct opposite to the witch community.

"Well, that's one thing in his favor," I said. "Do you want dessert?"

We decided on lava cake a la mode and moved on to discussing my flowered walkway and Bree's hectic summer schedule.

BY THE TIME WE FINISHED, it was six-fifteen. I asked Bree if she wanted to come back with me to help me plant flowers, but she had to sort out her schedule for the upcoming week.

"I'll be gone Friday through Sunday on a trip. I'm leading a hike into the Olympics. It's an easy-access trip. We'll leave Friday morning and be back Sunday afternoon. I doubt if I'll

have great cell service while I'm there." She paused by her car
—a full-size SUV that could take off-road gravel paths with
ease. "Give me a call tomorrow, if you can."

I nodded, waving as she drove away. As I fastened my seat
belt and headed toward home, I smelled a shift in the wind.
Rain was on its way.

TEN MINUTES LATER, I pulled into my driveway. A long
graveled road, the drive was a quarter mile long, winding
through a heavily wooded thicket. Firs and birch trees lined
the road, and the undergrowth was so thick that once I
started my trail project, I would need a machete to create a
path.

I slowed as I drove along the gravel road, through the
copse of trees, into the clearing.

The cottage maintained a fairytale look, and it was truly a
witch's cottage. It reminded me of an English cottage, sans
the thatched roof. Shingles lasted longer, in my opinion, and I
was relieved that the prior owner had agreed.

Built in the early 1920s, it had been renovated through the
years. With around sixteen hundred square feet, the cottage
had three bedrooms. One of my deal breakers had been a
basement, so I'd been relieved to find none during my first
visit. Basements creeped me out. The cottage was single
story, but it suited my needs.

The siding was in good condition, painted a pale sage
green with white trim. Built-in raised flower boxes
surrounded the base of the house. They were empty at this
point, but I wanted something perennial for them—something that didn't die off for six to nine months of the year.

A huge oak tree stood in back of the cottage on the left,
shading it with solemn solidity. To the right was a weeping

willow, massive with low-hanging branches. The drive circled around a water fountain that had seen better days, but it stopped directly in front of the house. The walkway had been overgrown, a faint trail through the knee-high grass when I first bought the place, but I'd weeded and cleared the slate walk.

A white picket fence cordoned off the cottage from the driveway, and I'd cut back the grass, and now the cottage and the yard looked cozy and tidy. The slate walk curved around the side of the house over to the workshop—which was about fifteen yards away—and the utility shed—another twenty yards from the workshop.

The picket fence was in reasonably good shape, and I'd refreshed the paint except where a thick patch of blackberries had overgrown a ten-foot section. I liked that, so I left them there, though I knew they'd eventually destroy the slats beneath it.

Tidying up the immediate yard around the house and workshop had taken me two months, but each day I managed to reclaim a little more from the hands of time and nature that had encroached, and now the cottage had truly become home.

The cottage had three bedrooms. The second largest I had made my library/office. The smallest, I'd turned into a guest room. The last, the master bedroom, was mine, of course. It had a decent-size walk-in closet and a cozy bathroom with a walk-in shower.

The country kitchen had room enough for a small table and four chairs. There was no dining room, but the living room was fairly large. The powder room in the short hall that led to the bedrooms was a two-piece—toilet and sink. The wood stove was in the living room. It was modern, air-tight, and I'd had the chimney replaced and fully inspected.

Turning off the ignition, I parked in front of the arched

trellis that led to the slate sidewalk, and decided that, before unloading the flowers, I'd light a fire before the night chill came on.

Glancing to my left and right, I slung my purse over my shoulder and dashed up to the door and unlocked it. The smell of stew hit me as I opened the door. I'd started it in the slow cooker before I left for town, and now the aroma of tomatoes and beef and gravy filled the air. I wasn't hungry now, but it would make for a good meal tomorrow. Maybe a good breakfast.

I dropped my purse on the console table next to the door, then headed over to the corner where the stove was. A pellet stove, it was designed so that it didn't need electricity to burn should the power go out. It was automatic, but it also had a manual setting and I'd decided to use that during the summer and set it to light automatically once autumn arrived. I turned on the stove and within a few minutes, the fire was crackling behind the glass.

Then, making sure the door was unlocked, I returned to the car and carried the flowers from the back over to set them on the ground along the walk, where I wanted to plant them.

After I finished, I glanced at the sky. Still no sign of rain, though I could feel it coming—a while out yet, but it was there. It was still light enough to see, but out in the country the night came earlier. I could hear the birds singing their evensong, and decided to call it a day.

MY NAME IS ELPHYRA MACPHERSON. I'm a witch by birth. My clan's known for being blood-connected to the elements so deeply that we're almost a part of them more than we are human. It's our destiny to hunt down the demons of the earth, regardless of their origin, and most of us answer the call willingly. We're magical by blood, detectable in the DNA, unlike the witches who choose the path. Their magic is a different sort—more kitchen witchery rather than full-fledged magic.

I was born in Port Townsend, and I lived there most of my life. I attended Port Townsend High, where I met Bree. After that, I entered Glendale College, a private four-year college. By the time I was twenty-two, I had my BA with primary studies in magical herbs and divination, along with a minor in botany, and promptly took a job with a plant nursery. I was managing the store within two years, and had worked there until a year ago.

I was working there when I met Rian and it was love at first sight. When I moved in with him, we talked about opening our own businesses—maybe an herb shop, and we could clear and bless houses on the side. I thought of hiring myself out as a magical gardener for those who wanted their gardens to have that extra-special feel. And if that wasn't lucrative, well, Port Townsend certainly had enough ghosts to go around. I was also good at reading cards and creating spells for people.

But then...everything crashed and I ended up back at home, lost in a mire of depression and PTSD. It's been a struggle to pull myself out, but now I'm okay. Mostly. So I took the trust fund my father left me—I hadn't touched it, planning on using it for later when Rian and I married—and I bought the cottage with three acres in Starlight Hollow. I did my best to say goodbye to Rian, and now, I'm determined to get on with my life and move into my future, instead of being chained by my past.

NEXT MORNING, the air was crisp and cool at seven A.M., and the echo of birdsong echoed through my yard. My land was mostly wooded with a few paths through the thicket, and a small stream—Juniper Creek—ran through the back half of it. Several clearings dappled the copse, and one of them I intended to turn into a grove.

I had decided to get up early and start in on the flowers before the day heated up. I was thinking about my great-grandmother's letter, still trying to figure a way to wiggle out of it, when a friendly voice hailed me.

"Elphyra! Good morning!"

I glanced over at one of the trailheads that was near my workshop. There, waving as she hustled my way was May, my neighbor. I sat back on my heels, smiling.

"Hey, May! What's up?" I stood, arching my back as I stretched. I was wearing a pair of black denim shorts and a green halter top.

"I brought you over your mail—the mail lady delivered it to me again." She pulled a packet of envelopes from the pocket of her apron.

May was in her late sixties and as active as I was. She wore her long silver hair in a ponytail, and she had on jeans and a floral button-up shirt. Her apron had a continuous row of deep pockets across the front. May was my closest neighbor. She owned Brambleberry Farm, the last house on the road.

"Thanks. I talked to her yesterday but I swear, she tunes out everything she doesn't want to hear." I took the packet and thumbed through the letters. Mostly junk mail, but there was a letter reminding me to renew my license tags, and another with my business license. I walked with May over to the front of the house as I opened that envelope.

"Look!" I held the paper up in front of her.

She took it and read, "Silver Thorns. A Magical Apothe-cary. Congratulations! I love the name."

"I do too. It's different and it stands out in a good way. I'm now legal to set up my magical practice. So, have a seat." The weatherproof benches were a find. I wanted to eventually build a deck out of the same material. I also had a rocking chair, a picnic table, and a grill. "Would you like some lemonade and cookies?"

"I ate, so I'm good for now," she said, sitting in the rocking chair. "I see you're adding color to the place. It's so beautiful here, and peaceful."

"I'm working on it," I said. "I still need to cast a protection spell over the whole place, and I need to enchant and bury crystals and obsidian arrowheads to enforce it." I stretched out my feet, crossing them at the ankles.

"Are you glad you moved here?" May asked.

I nodded. "I think I am. It's beautiful. I wanted peace and quiet, though I didn't realize how quiet it was going to be. But I can live with that."

After a moment, May said, "Starlight Hollow's going to have a street fair tonight. You should think about going."

When May made a suggestion, I usually followed it. From the first time she showed up at my door, I trusted my instincts about her. She was a kitchen witch. She wasn't born with it in her blood, but she had a knack and she was strong with the Sight. The spellcraft that kitchen witches practiced was considered basic, but in truth, theirs was the foundation for all of the stronger magical systems, based on a connection with all the elements, but especially with the earth beneath our feet.

"Maybe I will. I wonder if Bree's going. I'll give her a call." I took a deep breath. "It smells like rain. I smelled it yesterday, too. It will be here before dawn." I closed my eyes, feeling the moisture as it began to cluster and call to the clouds.

"Oh, rain will definitely be here before dawn tomorrow. I

can feel it in my bones. I may still be active, but my joints always tell me the truth." May motioned to the flowers waiting to be planted. "Would you like some help?"

"You don't have to offer—" I started to say, but she waved away my protest.

"I wouldn't offer if I didn't want to." She pulled a trowel out of her apron. "See, I came prepared!"

I couldn't argue with that.

As we settled down on the ground next to the walkway and dug into the soil, I hesitated for a moment, then said, "Bree says you're completely trustworthy and that I can believe you."

"Bree's right," May said. "I've found that life is easier if you tell the truth and stick to your principles. That's the way I brought my son up."

I nodded. I hadn't had a chance to meet her son yet, not in the few months I'd lived here, but I figured when it was time, I would. "Is he back yet?"

"Yes, Bran's back. He arrived home a month ago."

Bran had been away for a couple months traipsing around Europe, I gathered. He had gone with his girlfriend, May told me, and they had gone the backpack and hostel route.

"Did he have fun? Is he glad to be home?"

"He is. But the engagement is off." May didn't sound all that upset.

"What happened? It's none of my business, but...hadn't they been engaged for a couple years?" I couldn't imagine leaving Rian. It had taken death to divide us, but not everybody was lucky enough to have that kind of love in their lives.

May sighed, sitting back, resting on her hands as she turned her face toward the sun. "Apparently, Gloria decided she wanted to see the world in a more expansive way. Four weeks in, she tried to convince Bran to move to Paris. But as much as he enjoyed visiting, he wasn't interested in leaving the farm—and me—behind."

"From what you've told me, I can't imagine him agreeing to that," I said. Every word May had said about Bran indicated that they had a healthy, loving mother–son relationship.

"He didn't. So Gloria decided to have a Parisian fling with some guy they met in a club. Bran caught her in the back, naked with Julien. Bran divided their money and her return ticket, and set out to explore through Europe on his own. He didn't tell me they'd broken up until he returned. He didn't want me to worry."

"He sounds devoted to you," I said.

"He's a good son. He runs our suburban farm and keeps the bees happy, and during winter, he does the odd job here and there. I hope he finds a good woman who will be happy being a farmer's wife." She sparkled when she talked about him.

"How old is he?" I asked, patting the dirt around another primrose.

"He's thirty-five. How old are you, dear?"

"Thirty-three." I wondered if she'd had him later in life. Though she didn't look it, May appeared to be around seventy. "I was born on November first."

"Samhain proper," she said.

"Yeah. My mother said that's a sure sign I'm going to make a difference in the world. But I don't give credence to wives' tales like that." I tapped another primrose out of the container it was in and settled it into the new hole I'd dug. The smell of growing things made me happy—it calmed me like nothing else.

At that moment, a car pulled up my driveway. It was the sheriff's car.

"What's Daisy doing here?" May asked, a concerned look

on her face. She stood. "Daisy Parker is our sheriff—she's a puma shifter, so watch yourself."

As I scrambled to my feet, a tall, lithe woman stepped out of the car. She looked good in her uniform, but one look at her expression told me she was all business.

"May! Bran said I could find you here." The sheriff walked across the lawn to where we were standing.

"Daisy, what's wrong?" May asked.

"It's Olivia. She's been murdered."

And just like that, my home went from a safe haven to reminding me that no place was safe.

CHAPTER THREE

MAY GASPED. "OLIVIA? OLIVA *WORTH*?"

"I'm so sorry," Sheriff Parker said. "I know she was a good friend of yours."

"Olivia was murdered? Are you sure?" May stumbled back a step and I braced her by the shoulders. "What on earth happened?"

I gently led May over to one of the benches and motioned for the sheriff to follow us. "Have a seat, please."

The sheriff looked at me. "How do you do, ma'am? I'm Sheriff Daisy Parker. You're new in town, correct? Bree's friend?"

"Bree Loomis? Yes, she's my best friend. We've known each other since high school," I said. "And yes, I'm Elphyra MacPherson. I moved here from Port Townsend about five months ago."

"Good to meet you." She held out a hand and I shook it. "I'm sorry we have to meet under these circumstances, but life is what it is." The sheriff turned to May. "Again, I'm so sorry to be the bearer of bad news."

"What happened? Who killed her?"

"That we don't know, in terms of who the murderer is. As to what happened..." She pulled out a tablet, looking uncertainly at May. "This is pretty graphic..."

"You know I'm made of stern stock," May said. She straightened. "I can take it. You caught me by surprise."

Still looking hesitant, the sheriff raised her tablet. If she had pictures on it, she didn't show either of us. "Olivia's daughter reported her missing yesterday. Since Olivia has several major health concerns, we sent out a search party. A neighbor reported that Olivia had told her she was going to go berry picking. Salmonberries and wild raspberries are in season. She wasn't home when her daughter Lani arrived for dinner."

"Lani's a good girl. She loves her mother." May's voice was strained.

"Yes, well, she has a key to her mother's house, so she was able to get in. She found no sign of her mother, but Olivia's purse was there, as was her car, though her wallet and phone were missing. Lani was afraid that Olivia might have had a low blood sugar seizure, so she called her mother, but there was no answer. She let herself in and waited, calling every ten minutes. A half hour later, she called us."

"That's not like Olivia. She answers her phone religiously," May said.

"That's what Lani told us. We sent out a search and rescue team to the berry patches near Olivia's home—there are two major picking spots. The search dogs picked up on her scent and followed the track deeper into the woods, where they found...what's left of her." The sheriff winced. "She was... It's not going to be an open casket."

I paled, queasy. May surprised me, remaining stalwart and steady.

"Could she have been attacked by an animal?" I asked.

"We thought so at first, but the coroner says no. She was

literally torn to pieces. Somebody went ape-shit crazy on her." The sheriff shook her head. "We'll know more when the full autopsy is finished. Meanwhile, May, I was wondering if you know whether Olivia had any enemies?"

May frowned, thinking. "Everybody loved Olivia. I mean, *everybody*. I don't think the woman ever rubbed anybody the wrong way. Although she won every pie baking contest at the fair, no one ever begrudged her the accolades. Even me. Winning the preserve category's enough for me."

"What about her daughter?" the sheriff asked. "We have to check out relatives first."

"No, absolutely not. Lani loves her mother. There's scant to inherit. Olivia has never had much money. Just her house, and Lani's house is nicer than that. I know that the girl had some problems when she was younger—she ended up in rehab," May said. "But she's been clean and sober for years."

As I listened to them, an odd feeling crept over me—a dark shadow that lurked just out of sight. I wasn't sure if it was a premonition, or my own reaction to the violence.

"Elphyra?"

Startled, I realized that the sheriff was talking to me. "I'm sorry, I was thinking."

"I was wondering if you have any scrying abilities? May helps us out at times, but we could use a fully trained psychic or witch in town again. It's been awhile." She was staring at me, her eyes a striking hazel color.

I blinked. "Actually, yes. I'm adept in divination and scrying. Why?"

"The last seer who lived in town was helpful to the department when we needed her. I thought..." She paused, then smiled.

I realized that she was asking me, without asking, if I'd volunteer to help out. While I could say no, I knew I'd been recruited. Given I was new in town and wanted to make a good impression, I decided to roll with it. Crossing the police was never a good thing.

"Sure. If I can help, just ask." I cleared my throat. "For what it's worth, I felt an odd shadow appear when you were talking about the murder. I warn you, I have PTSD, so I'm not sure if it was anxiety over the thought of Olivia's death, or if it's something else." I wanted to lay all my cards on the table. I had no intention of leading the sheriff on a wild goose chase.

Daisy Parker simply nodded. "We all carry baggage. I'll take that into account. Can you describe the feeling?"

I shrugged. "I'm not sure—as I said, it felt like a dark shadow. Anger, I think. Or maybe...I don't know. Resentment, maybe? Or...hunger?" I closed my eyes but the energy had retreated.

After a moment, the sheriff stood. "I've taken up enough of your time. Thank you. And May, I am truly sorry."

"Daisy, Olivia never made an enemy. At least, not as long as I've known her," May said. "Whoever did this couldn't have been a personal enemy."

"Chances are, it was a murder of opportunity. But we'll know more later." She tucked the tablet under her arm. "I'll talk to you later, May." Inclining her head to me, she added, "Nice to meet you, Elphyra. Welcome to Starlight Hollow." Turning on her heel, she headed back to her car.

I STOOD THERE, uncertain what to do next. "Are you all right?" I asked May.

She glanced at the sky. "Such dark news for such a bright day. I'll miss Olivia. She's—she was one of my oldest friends here." She dashed away a tear, frowning. "But I've lived through worse, my dear. I'll manage." Motioning to the flowers, she said, "Let's get back to planting. Let's bring life into the world in memory of Olivia."

I followed her back to the walkway and we sat down on the ground again, returning to our task. I shivered, suddenly chilly in the warm morning air.

"If you feel like telling me, you can, you know," May said after a moment.

I raised my head. She didn't have to spell it out. I knew exactly what she was talking about. "Maybe. I don't know."

"You're going to have to talk about it at some point. You might as well get it out in the open. The tension surrounds you like a cloud." She wiped her hands on a rag and leaned back. "Why did you leave Port Townsend? You froze when Daisy said Olivia was torn to pieces. It's horrible, yes, but reality often is."

I leaned back, knees to my chest as I wrapped my arms around them. "All right. I suppose it was wishful thinking to hope that I could avoid it—that I could consign the memories to the past. I guess you can't ever make things disappear by ignoring them."

"What happened to you, girl?" May asked, her gaze fastened on my face.

I stared back at her. "A year ago, in early April—April third, to be exact—Rian, my fiancé, and I went to a movie. After that, we stopped at a local bar to hang out with friends for an hour or so. By the time we left, it was dark and we were both tipsy. So we decided to walk home. The apartment we shared was only a mile away."

"What time was it?" May asked.

"Five past midnight. We had to cross through a questionable part of town, but in Port Townsend the seedy section only took up a couple blocks. We passed by an alley and the next thing I knew, somebody jumped out and grabbed hold of me. He was strong—so strong—and when Rian started toward us, he told him to come quietly or he'd slit my throat. I couldn't break his hold and I was too drunk to cast a spell."

I closed my eyes, trying to block out the flood of emotion that was threatening to drown me. But then, I was right back there—in the middle of it—and everything was all too crystal clear.

WHOEVER HAD hold of me was tall—at least six inches taller by what I could tell. He smelled like a popular men's cologne —Ice Flow. I didn't see a knife, but the command in the man's voice was impossible to ignore and I quit fighting and let him drag me into the shadows. The next thing I knew, Rian was there, his hands up.

"We don't want any trouble—we'll give you everything we have. Please don't hurt her. Let us go, and we won't go to the police."

But the man didn't seem interested in robbing us because he pointed toward an open door against the wall of a rundown building.

"In there," he said, ordering Rian in first. Then he shoved me through and shut the door behind him.

We were standing in a dim room, lit by a single bare bulb hanging from the ceiling. There were no windows that we could see—perhaps they had been boarded over, or maybe they didn't exist. From where we stood I could see a dingy bathroom and a mattress in the corner. I couldn't see a kitchen. The only other thing I saw was a lumpy sofa against one wall. I also saw a few rats skittering around. My alarm bells went off, sounding *Danger! Danger!*

"I have a diamond ring—if you want it, it's yours." I held up my engagement ring.

But the man ignored it. "Sit over there," he said, pointing

to the sofa. He was holding a knife, a large one, smears of dried blood staining the blade.

We sat. I thought about charging him, but one stab of that knife and he'd gut me.

"Choose."

I glanced at Rian, then back at him. "What do you mean, choose?"

"One to watch and live, one for me to play with. *Choose.*" Again the snarl, and this time, I caught sight of his fangs. *Vampire.* Bad, bad news for us. Vampires were deadly. With few exceptions, they had little to offer mortals except death and danger. There were petitions out for vampire rights, but until they agreed to interact with us instead of using us as juice boxes, few people were sympathetic to their cause.

"You can't be serious—" Rian started, but the vamp cut him off.

"Oh, I'm deadly serious. If *you* don't choose, I'll choose for you." The vampire's eyes were gleaming, the irises snow white against the jet of his eyes. They were circled with crimson.

Beside me, Rian grabbed my hand and squeezed tight. He whispered, "I love you" and then said, "Me. Whatever you're going to do, do it to me."

"No—" I tried to hold him back, but Rian jumped to his feet. "Rian, no! You can't—"

"Don't listen to her. Whatever you're going to do, do it to me," he said. "Don't hurt her. Let her live, please. Do whatever you want to me, but don't hurt her. I beg of you." He fell to his knees before the vampire, pleading.

I whimpered, unable to control my fear.

Rian turned back to me. "You will live, you'll make it through this. I love you—don't ever forget that I love you, and I always will."

A stark thought that he knew he was going to die crossed

my mind and I fell into silence, unable to process what was going on.

The vampire let out a husky laugh. "I thought so, though you might be surprised. The last pair, the man shoved his wife into my arms." He shrugged. "No matter to me, but...at least you're a *real* man and I respect that, as much as I respect any blood bag." He held up a pair of handcuffs and motioned for Rian to move against one of the walls. "You stand there until I'm ready for you, or I'll do such exquisite things to her that you'll never wipe her screams from your memories."

Rian crossed over to the wall and stood there, head down. I wanted to plead with him, to beg him to change his mind, but I knew that look. Rian wasn't going to change his mind. He was a Renaissance man, and he loved with his whole heart.

I was shaking so hard that the vampire had to grip my wrists to slip the cuffs on me. He draped the chain connecting the cuffs over a hook on the wall above me so that my hands were over my head and I was forced to sit at full attention.

I mouthed "I love you" to Rian and he blew me a kiss.

My heart racing, I recoiled as the vamp ran a finger along my chin, sniffing my neck.

"I can hear your heart—it's filled with blood," he whispered. "Your pulse is racing, your heart galloping, like a horse in the wind. Do you know how inviting that is to me? How hard it makes me? I would love to slide my fangs into your neck and drink deep."

I was trying to calm myself, to keep myself from hyperventilating. The next moment, he said, "But I'm a man of my word. Just a taste, that's all." He leaned closer and, tongue snaking out, licked my neck with one long stroke. I grimaced, trying to turn away. He caught hold of my chin and forced me to look into his eyes. I fell into their depths, trying to look away, but the vamp's glamour held me fast.

"Listen to me. You will watch every move I make. You'll take it all in. You can't shut your eyes for more than a blink. You'll remember every detail. You'll never be able to forget me or what you see here tonight." His words echoed in my mind, like a bullet ricocheting from one side to another. "You understand?"

I nodded, unable to speak. He abruptly withdrew and—as I froze—he crossed to Rian. As I watched, he tore off Rian's shirt, then bit deep into his neck, the sound of tearing flesh echoing through the room. The blood raced down the vamp's pale chin. Rian moaned, his head lolling back as a river of red gushed down his chest. He whimpered, his eyes filling with pain and with passion.

I tried to look away, but I was condemned to watch as the vampire ravaged my fiancé, making Rian beg for more, even as he was screaming due to the pain. Next, he bit Rian's wrists and then tore away the rest of his clothing. As he knelt in front of my love, I tried to scream, but I couldn't force a sound from my throat. Then, the torture began in earnest, with the vamp using both his rusty blade and his fangs.

Every detail burned a memory into my brain, the images all too clear and vivid.

Rian didn't die easily. By the time the vamp was done, my future and my heart were on the floor in front of me, a bloody mess of flesh and blood that had once been a man. I vomited more than once, and when the vampire came toward me after he was done, I expected to follow Rian into death. But he wrinkled his nose, recoiling at the scent as he undid my handcuffs.

"Listen to me, girl. You'll sit here until sunrise creeps through the papers on the window, and then you'll be free to go. I told you, I'm a man of my word. But...one day—some day in the future, when you least expect it—I'll return for you. I'll come back and we'll have our fun. That, I also promise you. I always keep track of my toys." And with that, he unlocked the cuffs, then slipped out the door, shutting it behind him.

Still paralyzed, I sat there, unable to move as the rats moved in on Rian's body. And finally, a thousand years later, a beam of light crept through a hole in the boards that were covering the window, and I was free of the glamour. I grabbed my phone and dialed 911 before I descended into the darkness.

MAY STARED AT ME, her face ashen. She said nothing, but stood and motioned for me to follow her. We crossed through a path in the woods, still silent, till we came out near a two-story farmhouse. Brambleberry Farm.

It was older, like my home, but she had kept it in good shape. I followed her up the porch and through the front door. Although I'd met her several times, it had always been at my place.

I glanced around as we entered the house. A living room sat to the right, a parlor to the left. The hallway led past a stairwell leading up, and a closed door next to it. To the right of the stairwell was a large country kitchen–dining room, where she led me. Beyond the kitchen was a mudroom, and I thought I could see a utility room from where I stood.

"Sit down," she said, putting the kettle on the combo electric–wood cookstove. She brought out a loaf of fresh bread, some butter, and honey. "I want you to eat something. After that story, you have to be drained."

I obediently spread butter and honey on a thick slice of bread and bit into it. She was right. I needed something to shore me up. I was drained. Every time I thought about that night, the vamp's orders that everything would remain crystal clear remained intact, and it was as though I relived it with every telling. I'd managed to get to the point where I stopped crying, mostly, but that was scant consolation.

"Tell me, have you seen anybody about helping you remove those triggers he implanted in you?" she asked.

"What do you mean? What triggers?"

"Vampires have a number of special powers. He was probably able to latch onto those memories and encrypt them with a biological response. It's like you're right there again, isn't it?" She poured two cups of peppermint tea and handed one to me, sitting down at the end of the table.

I nodded. "Yeah, how did you know?"

"I know all too much about vampires," she said. "I learned the hard way. Not as hard as you did, but it was no picnic. And I had to find a way to break that connection. I was sick of having him inhabit my head and feed on me. They can, you know—if you're linked like that, a vampire can feed off of your energy and play the leech. You're feeding him every time you think of that night. At least right now."

Horrified, I stared at her. "How do I stop it? I don't want his filthy fangs on me, not in *any* way!"

"We can break it, but I need to know more about him, if you have any clue. First, though, eat and recharge yourself. I feel like I should apologize for making you relive that terrible night. I can't believe the cops didn't advise you to seek help for it."

"Maybe they didn't know about the connections," I muttered. Port Townsend's police force wasn't a joke, but vampires weren't all that common, although the latest news said that they were on the increase.

"Bullshit. All law enforcement agencies know about vampires, though they don't always admit it. The menace is growing, and it's not going to go away. Not unless the government gets off its ass and organizes a task force focused on keeping tabs on the vamps." She frowned. "Daisy was new at her job when I had my encounter."

"What happened to you?" I asked. "If I can ask?"

"My nephew was turned by a vampire. He came here, looking to turn Bran and me. We managed to fight him off. I know a good deal of lore about keeping vampires at bay and I happen to have an herb cabinet to rival the best herb store in town. You can always ask me if I have something before going shopping for it, by the way," she added.

I regarded her silently. If May had managed to fight off a vampire, then she was stronger than I thought she was. "How did you scare him off?"

"Good old folk magic. The minute I knew he had been turned, I strung garlic around every door and window. I also cast a mirror spell, deflecting him away from the house. He showed up but couldn't get through and I took that time to revoke his invitation to enter my house. The next day, Bran and I walked the entire length of the property, warding it against vampires."

"Is he still out there?" I asked.

She nodded. "Yes. If we could have, we would have staked him. But neither Bran nor I were ever afforded the opportunity. I have no idea where he is, but I'm hoping that he went far away."

"Can you help me ward my property the same way?" I took a sip of the peppermint tea, letting the cool mint rush through my thoughts.

"I can. Do you know his name?"

I shook my head. "I don't know his actual name, but he's on the list of the top ten nation's Most Wanted Vampires—the list bounty hunters go by. He's called the 'Choose Your Poison Butcher.' We were the eighteenth couple he targeted in eight years. He's been all across the nation."

"What about those who survived?" May asked.

"The first two survivors were killed in the same way, a number of years after their ordeals. Authorities think he returns to finish them off. From what I understand, most of the current survivors have gone underground, but if what you're saying is true—if we're linked—maybe that's how he finds them." The thought of forever being on my guard, forever looking over my shoulder, rested heavy on my shoulders.

"Then it's imperative that we disconnect you from him," May said. "And that we set up a trap so that if he ever comes near you, he'll burn till he crisps."

And with that, she began to outline what we would need as I tried to drag myself out of my nightmarish past, into the present.

CHAPTER FOUR

MAY SAID THAT SATURDAY WOULD BE THE BEST TIME TO cast the spell, given it would be the new moon and it would hide what we were doing from the Butcher.

"I don't know if he can sense when something like that happens," she said. "But the new moon is the best time to take care of matters best hidden from others. Come over Saturday at four and we'll get started. For now, here—wear this around your neck." She handed me a hand-carved Algiz rune that smelled like an Italian restaurant. "I rubbed this with garlic oil and it will keep him away from you. The problem is, he could glamour you and force you to take off the charm, so you need to wear a smoky quartz pendant because that's the one crystal that has the chance to break a vampire's charm. Do you have one?"

I nodded. "Yes, I do. My mother gave it to me."

"Then wear it night and day until we can pull the plug on him." She glanced at the clock. "All right, I have to get to work. I have herbs to tend to, and Bran's coming home for lunch." She paused, then added, "Unless you'd like to stay and meet him?"

41

I hesitated. "It's not that I don't want to meet him, but I promised Bree I'd meet her this afternoon. She's closed on Tuesdays and Sundays, so we're going to meet for lunch and then she's going to introduce me to a couple of her clients who have been looking for a good tarot reader or something like that."

"Well then, that sounds good," May said. "I'll talk to you later."

I headed back to my place through the shortcut. The rune reeked of garlic and I tried to decide if I thought I was in enough danger to wear it out in public. I was terrified of the Butcher, but was he going to come after me so soon? That wasn't part of his MO. He usually let time enough go by so that his victims had let down their guard.

Then again, what better trick to play than let me believe it would be years before he showed up? What if he'd felt May's energy puttering around in the cords he left linked to me? I had no idea what might arouse suspicion in him. On the other hand, I might scare off potential clients. I finally decided to wear the smoky quartz pendant on a thick silver chain. The crystal, along with the silver, might be enough to deflect him.

There was a mirror on the back of my bedroom door and I checked out my reflection. I had slipped on a sundress— black with white trim. It had a ruched back panel that had stretch in it, gathered at the waist, then flared out into a full skirt that fell two inches above my knee. I added a silver belt, for good measure, then slid on a pair of ankle boots with stacked heels. As I laced them up, I thought again about my mother and pulled out my phone.

LOVE YOU. I'LL CALL SOON AND WE CAN HAVE A LONG CHAT. —E

Within seconds, she texted back, LOVE YOU TOO. TALK SOON.

BREE WAS WAITING for me at the restaurant. We were eating at Jam Jam's—a combo diner/takeout joint. You could order for pickup, through the takeout window, or sit inside.

The booths were minimalist—hard plastic, or at least I thought it was plastic. While they didn't encourage lingering, they weren't uncomfortable either, and the food made any lack of atmosphere worth it. Every bite was incredible. I ordered fish and chips and a strawberry milkshake. Bree ordered a burger, fries, and a chocolate shake, and we settled into one of the booths.

"So, how are you doing today? You seemed tense last night."

"I'm all right. I finally told May what happened to me." I sighed. "It had to happen some time. She thinks the Butcher still has hooks in me, so she's going to help me get rid of those cords on Saturday." I paused, looking around the diner. The walls and trim were pale blue, and there were hints of yellow and pink in the curtains and décor. The owners meant to mimic the morning sky, I thought. And on a subconscious level, it worked.

"Do you think I was a coward to leave Port Townsend?" I asked.

Bree shook her head. "You ran for a good reason. Sometimes you can be so immersed in something that you need to get out of it before you can see it clearly." She paused. "I wish you didn't have to deal with all that."

"Wrong place at the wrong time," I said. "Sometimes luck is against us."

The waitress brought over our meals and we dug in.

"So, tell me about these friends of yours. Anything I should stick clear of discussing? They aren't skeptics or wannabes, are they?" I hated reading for clients who were out to either prove me wrong, or who wanted to go home and squeal to their friends about how they met a *real witch* so they could be in with the cool kids.

"Neither. And I thought they might want readings, but by Darla's text, I think they want to talk to you about something else. Mother and daughter pair. Darla and Georgie—short for Georgina. Darla's family recently moved to town and their house is haunted. I'm not sure what they want from you, but can you at least hear them out?"

"What are you getting me into?" I asked. "Ghosts? I don't like dealing with ghosts!" But at her pleading look, I relented. "All right, I'll meet them." I bit into my fish and sighed happily. "Deep-fried fish. Is there anything better?"

"Fried chicken," Bree said, laughing.

"Well, maybe...okay, they're both right up there." I poured more ketchup on my fries. "Oh, I met the sheriff last night."

"How? What happened?"

I told her about the sheriff, and Olivia. "Apparently something tore her to pieces."

"That's scary. Poor May—I know they were good friends. Hold on," she said. "I think I heard about Olivia on the news." She pulled out her phone and flipped through the apps, finally bringing one up. A few more taps and she blanched as she stared at the screen.

"What is it? You've turned white as a sheet."

"There was another murder this morning." Bree looked up from her phone. "A man this time, torn to bits. He was found right outside of the town limits, on an access road leading into Olympic National Park across Highway 101."

"Did he live in Starlight Hollow?"

"Yes. His name was Lucius Jackaberry. He was thirty-two, and found in the same state that Olivia was." She paused, then added, "It says here that the attacks looked like they were made by an animal."

I said, taking a long sip of my milkshake.

"The coroner said that while Olivia's wounds were reminiscent of an attack by a pack of dogs, they were made by something else." She glanced up, frowning. "Apparently he now thinks a shifter did it. He says that if it had been a dog pack, they would have eaten parts of her, but nothing was... devoured...as far as they can tell."

"Shifter?" I stared at her. "A wolf shifter, maybe?" I didn't care for shifters, either—at least, not for wolf shifters. Unlike most of the other types of shifters, wolf shifters were staunchly averse to magic and they didn't trust witches. And because of that prejudice, we didn't trust wolf shifters either.

"I don't know. But given that he first thought it might be a pack of dogs, that would make sense. Shifters can do far more damage than the animals they're connected to. Hell, I'm a puma shifter and I'm a lot more dangerous than a regular mountain lion." She glanced around, then lowered her voice. "You know that the Olympic Wolf Pack is headquartered here. They live on the southwest side of town, near the highway. There's one big commune, and then a few individual residents."

"Do shifters always live in a communal situation?"

Bree shrugged. "I can't speak for other shifter groups, but I can tell you that the Kalaloch Puma Shifters don't. We prefer our privacy and we only gather for quarterly meetings at the headquarters of our Pride. If there are community emergencies, we may call a special assembly, but that only happens in the event of an emergency."

"Cripes, everything goes south so quickly. What happened to the carefree days of childhood?" I grumbled.

Laughing, Bree said, "They only existed in our minds. The adults knew what was going on, but they protected us from it." She finished her burger. "So, you ready to meet Darla and her daughter Georgie?"

"I guess so," I said, finishing the last French fry. "Where are we meeting?"

"Jitters 'n Bows." She paid the check and we headed toward the door. "Follow me?"

"See you there." I held up my keys and headed for my Chevy.

JITTERS 'N BOWS was one of the best coffee shops to ever grace the planet. Their coffee was incredible, their mochas and other espresso drinks were perfect, their brownies and cookies were to die for, and they were reasonably priced in an overinflated world.

We parked near the door and headed inside. While it was the most popular coffee shop around, ninety percent of their traffic was drive-thru, which meant getting a seat wasn't all that difficult. After we pushed through the door, Bree led the way over to a corner table where a couple of blondes were waiting.

They looked like mother and daughter, I thought. High-lighted wheat-colored hair, nails a perfect nude but nicely done, their makeup was similar, and they were both wearing blue jeans and crop tops. The mother—it had to be—had some crow's feet around her eyes, and her lips were creased as if she smoked, but otherwise, they could have been sisters.

"Darla, Georgie, hello," Bree said. "I promised and I deliv-ered. Meet Elphyra MacPherson. I told you about her."

"Do you cleanse haunted houses?" Darla asked, even as Georgie peppered me with queries about poltergeists and if they could physically hurt people.

"One question at a time," I said, holding up my hands. They both sounded frantic, but they quieted when I spoke.

"I'm sorry," Darla said. "We're desperate. I'm Darla Bainbridge, and this is my daughter, Georgie. We're in trouble, and we need help."

I settled into my seat.

"What do you want? I'll get it," Bree said.

"Triple tall sugar-free vanilla latte," I said. "Iced."

While Bree went to grab our drinks, I turned back to Darla and Georgie. "So, you suspect your house is haunted? What makes you think so?"

I was deliberately being aloof because I wanted to scare them off if they were in it for the thrills. So many people thought every creak meant an invader and every dust speck they caught on camera was a spirit orb.

To my surprise, Darla nodded. "We know it's haunted, and whatever is there wants us to get out. We have no clue what to do about it, and we didn't want to try anything on our own because I don't want to make the situation worse. When Bree mentioned that you were a witch and planned on opening up a shop here in Starlight Hollow, we asked if she could introduce us."

Before I could answer, Bree returned with our drinks.

Georgie set down her cookie next to her coffee cup and said, "Mom's right. We need real advice, from someone who can decipher what's going on. We don't trust phone psychics, and we've met a couple other people in town who claim to be mediums, but they seem like amateurs."

I could sense the fear behind their frenetic energy. "Why don't you tell me what's wrong."

Darla glanced at Georgie. "Well, we recently moved into an older home, and the minute we did, things started happening."

"What about when you looked at it?"

"Our real estate agent found it for us while we were on

47

vacation. We were worried we'd lose out so we had her make an offer and we did something stupid, since there's such a scramble for real estate. We waived the inspection." Darla sighed, embarrassed.

"Well, that's not ideal. But you knew that."

"Yeah. So, when we moved in, the activity started immediately. And my husband suddenly started acting strangely. He's more temperamental and he yells at the kids a lot. He never did before. I've asked him what's wrong and he won't answer."

"What else has been going on?" I was interested now.

"As a family, we've started arguing more, and it's usually over nothing. And the arguments escalate. The other night Kevin—my husband—blew up when I told him dinner was late. He slammed out the door and sulked in the shed all evening. I finally talked him into coming inside before bed, but I thought he was going to lose his shit."

"Is this the only time that's happened?" I asked.

"No, but never before we moved into this house. And it's more than that," Darla said. "The kids are afraid of him." She looked defeated.

"Kids? So, you have more kids than Georgie?" I asked.

"Georgie's my oldest."

"I'm twenty-four. Kevin's not my father, but he's Mary and Johnny's dad."

"Mary's fourteen, and John is eight," Darla said.

I thought about all the spirits I'd dealt with in my life. "You said other things have been happening. Give me some examples." I didn't want to implant suggestions in their heads, so I left the question open-ended.

Georgie stirred her coffee. "I thought I saw a man looking over my shoulder at me, in the mirror. I screamed but when I turned around, there was no one there. He looked angry."

"Johnny has also had a couple encounters," Darla added.

"He keeps thinking something is in his closet. I have to get his clothes out for him, he's so scared of opening the door. He also said he saw the door open on its own."

"Mary told me that something grabbed her ankle the other night and tried to pull her off the bed," Georgie said. "I didn't know what to say, so I told her that if she wanted to, she could come sleep in my bed. We share a room."

"*What?* You didn't tell me that," Darla said, her eyes widening.

"We all know how rough things are around the house right now—the kids can tell. They're not stupid. She asked me to keep it a secret because she's afraid that Kevin will yell at her and call her stupid." Georgie crossed her arms, frowning. "He never used to do that."

"Never used to do what?" I asked. "Yell at you?"

"Kevin was always supportive of us," Georgie said. "But now, he calls us stupid or useless. Mary and Johnny do their best to avoid him. They still love him, but they're afraid of him. So they talk to me."

"Why not *me?*" Darla asked.

"Because *you're* trying to spare them. You always tell them everything's going to be fine, and they *know* it's not fine. They know there's something in that house." Georgie shrugged. "They aren't stupid, just scared."

Darla blushed lightly. She ducked her head. "Will you come over to our house and see what's going on? We just want things to go back to normal."

Bree stared at me, an expectant look on her face.

I took a sip of my latte and then nodded. "I'll do my best. When would be the best time? I'd prefer to work at night when there's less interference with the spirit world."

"Kevin's not going to like it," Darla said, frowning. "Wait! He goes bowling on Wednesday nights. Can you come over tomorrow night? He's usually gone from around seven until eleven."

"That will work," I said, pulling out my phone. "Give me your name and number, please." As I took down her information, I thought this would be a good case to start out my business with.

BREE and I decided to stop at the street fair after our meeting with Georgie and Darla. The fair was like a farmers market on steroids. Artists had joined the produce and meat vendors, and while the fair took up all of one block—on both sides of the street, as well as down the middle of it—there was plenty to choose from.

I was craving fresh vegetables, and there were plenty to be had. I wasn't that interested in the jewelry vendors—not because I didn't like jewelry, but because my mind was running over what Darla and Georgie had told me. I picked through the vegetables, buying several cucumbers, a big bag of tomatoes, some carrots, a bag of red potatoes, and a flat of strawberries.

"Did you want some honey?" Bree asked as we crossed through the aisles of vendors.

The Gig Harbor BeeMan sold his honey here, along with a couple other smaller beekeepers. It was raw, with bits of honeycomb in it, and I had developed a taste for it.

I bought a quart of it, and Bree bought some refined honey and a few of his beeswax candles. We then stopped at the Cookie Lady's stall. She made huge cookies, in a dozen different kinds, and I bought three of her chocolate peanut-butter chip cookies. Each one was five inches in diameter. She also sold cinnamon and pecan rolls, and fresh bread, so I bought a loaf of her French bread, while Bree bought a half-dozen pecan rolls. The Cookie Lady was tall and sturdy, with long blond braids and she wore maxi-skirts and tank tops. Nobody knew what her real name was. We all called her Cookie.

As we were nearing the end of the street, I spotted one of the flower merchants. "Look, they have the first batches of hyacinths." I bought a big bouquet and buried my face in them as we turned around. "I love the scent—"

The next thing I knew, I was on the ground with all my purchases. My honey jar had broken and was running a sticky mess on the street. Bree was leaning over me.

"Are you all right?"

I nodded, flustered, not sure of what had happened. "I... what the hell?"

It was then that I noticed a tall man standing to one side, scowling at me. He had honey on his shirt. "Watch where you're going, *witch*," he said. It was then that I noticed his scent—like cloves. He smelled good, but there was something beneath the surface... *Oh good gods*, he was a *wolf* shifter. I knew that scent, because it came out like skunk spray when they were irritated. It was musky and dry.

I scrambled to my feet. "It takes two to tango, you know," I said, scowling back. Bree was picking up the rest of my purchases, but the flowers were also a casualty. They'd been crushed when I fell. I'd landed on them. "Look what you did to my hydrangeas and my honey!"

"If you'd been looking where you were going, you wouldn't have run into me. You ruined my shirt," the man said. "I suppose you're going to deny that it was your fault?"

I glared at him, unable to look away.

He had long brown hair, pulled back in a ponytail, and eyes so dark they were like midnight coffee. I couldn't help but notice that he was also muscled beneath the T-shirt he was wearing. Snug jeans and a pair of hiking boots completed the outfit. I placed him about thirty-five or more, but it was impossible to tell for sure, given that shifters lived longer than humans or magic-blood.

"I *always* take responsibility for my actions. But you could be a bit more gracious about it." I didn't want to leave the glass on the ground. Luckily, the flower vendor brought over a dustpan and broom and a hose. I started to take them from her, but Bree arrived first and knelt beside the broken glass.

The wolf shifter still continued to watch me.

"Well, are you going to say something or burn a hole in me?" I said, irritated. I wasn't sure why, but everybody around us was staring as though they were waiting for the other shoe to drop. "I'm not going to get in a fight with you."

"I thought we were already arguing," he said, a sarcastic grin spreading across his face.

"Oh, shut the fuck up."

He snorted, then turned to the flower man and motioned to the hydrangea bouquets. The vendor silently handed one to him. The wolf shifter turned back to me and then suddenly reached out, stuffing the bouquet in my arms, along with a twenty-dollar bill.

"You have reparations. Go buy yourself some more honey. Maybe it will sweeten your disposition. And I'm *busy*, so if you'll excuse me..." He turned and strode away, leaving me once again, speechless.

Bree waited until he'd gone, then turned to me. "I hope you realize that's not the best person to mix it up with."

"Why? Who does he think he is?" I asked, still irritated.

"That's Faron Collinsworth, the King of the Olympic Wolf Pack." She laughed. "You just embarrassed one of the major power players in Starlight Hollow."

As I watched him go, all I could think was, "Oh, crap. What the hell was I thinking?" And yet, his image lingered in my mind. He was annoying as fuck, yes...but there was something about him.

"No." I shook my head.

"What?" asked Bree.

"Nothing," I said, refusing to let thoughts of Faron Collinsworth linger.

CHAPTER FIVE

I HUNG THE GARLIC CHARM OVER THE TOP OF MY BED AND
fell asleep the minute my head hit the pillow. But around two
A.M., I woke up abruptly, as though someone had shaken me
out of my sleep. I propped myself up on my elbows, listening.

The sounds of the night filtered through the screened but
open window. Straining my ears, I tried to pinpoint what had
startled me awake, but I couldn't tell if there had been a
sound or if it was just a feeling or a dream that had catapulted
me out of sleep.

Pushing back the blanket, I slipped on my robe over my
nightgown and slid my feet into a pair of moccasins. Flashlight in hand, I headed through the living room, unlocked the
door, and stepped out into the night.

Without the glare of city lights, the stars were shim-
mering overhead. I caught my breath at the beauty of the vast
expanse before turning my attention to figuring out what had
caught my attention. Once again, I reached out, trying to
sense where the disruption had come from. Whatever it was,
was hiding inside the treeline, off the path leading to May's
farm.

I paused, sussing out the energy. I couldn't sense a negative attachment to it. More...a certain amount of confusion, fear, and hunger.

I frowned, hoping it wasn't a cougar. While Bree was my best friend, a puma shifter and an actual puma were entirely different. I had no desire to end up on a big kitty-cat's menu, and wild animals seldom gave off negative or evil vibes. But most of the mountain lions—also known as pumas and cougars around here—wouldn't attack unless you made yourself look like prey.

As I neared the treeline, I turned on the flashlight and burst out in a loud, off-key version of "We Will Rock You." Noise would drive off most of the bigger predators. But I heard no sound of bushes rustling, or anything scrambling out of the way. And the feelings I had tuned into were still there, the fear growing stronger.

I set foot on the trail. Two yards in and I made a sharp left, cautiously stepping off the path and into the dense undergrowth. I brushed a spider's web out of the way, testing each step as I went. The woods in western Washington were often shin-deep in the detritus of years past, the compost thick with leaves, fir and cedar needles, and rotting bark that made up the rich loam of the forest. It was easy to turn an ankle or trip over a root, especially in the dark.

Whatever it was, I was closing in on it. The sensation of fear and confusion echoed in my head, like on a radar, the blip growing larger with each step I took.

I hadn't had time to fully explore the forest yet—I hadn't been here long enough, and I'd been so busy planting in flowers and getting my workshop set up. I paused at one point, swinging my flashlight right and left, examining my surroundings.

Up ahead, a nurse log blocked the way. Nurse logs were fallen timber—usually the huge firs that made up a good share of the forests around here. As they decayed, they became home to mushrooms and moss, to insects and small creatures that burrowed inside the massive trunks. Whatever I was sensing was right in front of me, somewhere in the log.

I approached the tree and knelt to examine it. To the right, an opening led into a hollow. I cautiously leaned in and pointed the beam of light into the hole. There, I saw something I'd never seen before. It was an egg—as large as an ostrich egg and a pale cranberry color. The egg was nestled in a thick pile of compacted leaves.

Frowning, I set the light down and gingerly reached into the hole, taking hold of the egg with both hands. The shell was warm—almost as warm as my own body. Curious, I brought out the egg and held it up.

"I've never seen anything like you," I said.

Ping... It was as though my words had touched whatever was inside the egg. I thought about putting it back, but everything in my instincts screamed "No!" and I had learned the hard way to pay attention to them. I shed my robe and after wrapping it around the egg, I stood. Carefully cradling it in my left arm, I picked up the flashlight and retraced my steps.

When I returned to the house I locked the door behind me. Then, turning on the light, I settled down at the desk in the living room to examine what I'd found.

The egg was just that—as far as I could tell. An egg. As I had first thought, it was about the size and shape of an ostrich egg, and now that I was inside, the color was more of a washed-out crimson with gold streaks.

"What bird lays eggs that look like this?" I couldn't imagine how big the bird would have to be. I took a picture and uploaded it to FindPlease—a new search engine that also had a reverse image search. None of the results remotely came close to matching. I tried again, taking a picture from a different angle.

This time, two links appeared. I clicked on one, and it was a child's drawing of a "baby dragon egg" on someone's family website. The other was more promising. It was from a cryptozoology site and it, too, said that the egg they found was a dud, but when they opened it up, they found what looked like the remains of an in-utero dinosaur-type bird:

It's thought that eggs like these may be the remains of a dragonette—one of the smallest members of the Drakon family, which includes dragons and dragon shifters. Dragonettes, unlike dragons, are the size of a large raven and they're the only member of the Drakon family that deliberately seeks out the company of humans. It's believed that dragonettes, like all members of the Drakon family, exist in an interdimensional state. When they're born, they're larva, but after a period of time, they spin a cocoon—basically the egg—and during their time in the egg, they fully mature. Like a butterfly breaking free of the chrysalis, they emerge fully aware and ready to live their life.

"Dragonettes? Seriously? It couldn't be. Not here." Though the egg on the screen looked similar to mine, I couldn't believe that I had a dragonette egg in front of me.

I closed the laptop and turned my attention back to the egg. Placing my hands on the shell, lightly so as not to damage it, I closed my eyes.

Again the feeling of confusion and fear hit me. Worried for whatever was inside, I wondered if the mama—whatever she was—had wandered off and forgotten about her egg. She'd have to be pretty large to pop out an egg like this. There were no birds around here large enough to squeeze out something of this size. Or were there? I wrapped the egg back in my robe and then searched on "eagle eggs." There were some pretty freaking huge eagles out there. But none popped out an egg the size of one sitting in front of me. A quick look at ostrich eggs placed the one I had found as slightly bigger than a large ostrich egg.

"So, unless we have an ostrich running around that lays odd-colored eggs, this is something completely different," I said, leaning back. Maybe it *was* a dragonette? But that still sounded so far-fetched to me.

It occurred to me that the egg was probably chillier than it had been in the nurse log, and I thought about tucking it into bed with me. But what if there was some sort of snake or spider or insect inside? I didn't relish waking up in bed next to something creepy-crawly. I could tuck it near the wood-stove, but I didn't want to accidentally cook whatever was inside.

But what if I kept it wrapped in my robe? If it hatched, the material might hinder the baby...whatsit...when it tried to peck its way out of the shell. It also occurred to me that the baby would be hungry and—until I knew what it was—I wouldn't have a clue what to have on hand to feed it.

"Well, I'll have to do my best." I emptied a drawer out of my dresser and lined it with towels. Then I loosely wrapped a pillowcase around the egg and put the drawer near enough the woodstove so that it would get reflected heat, but not close enough to roast. After that, I glanced at my phone. It was two-thirty, and I climbed back in bed, settling down as sleep once again closed over me.

✳

WITH EARLY MORNING came a blanket of mist rolling along the ground. The clouds had rolled in during the latter half of the night, and the ground was wet. It must have poured after my late-night jaunt. A sprinkle of rain was still spitting from the sky. I turned on the pellet stove and then took a warm shower to wake myself up. It was early—seven-thirty—and I wasn't sure why my body thought it needed to get up now, but awake I was.

As I lathered up with vanilla–musk shower gel, my thoughts drifted with my hands. It had been over a year since I lost Rian. I ran my hands lightly over my breasts, but all I could think of was how much I missed Rian's touch. I missed his arms around me, his lips on mine. It had been so long since he'd touched me.

The few times I turned to the toys in my nightstand to relieve my hunger, I'd ended up sobbing when I came, the images of the Butcher torturing him filling my thoughts. To say I was pent-up was an understatement. So I dealt with the frustration and tried to keep myself busy.

I dressed in my leather jeans and a light long-sleeved top, then blow-dried my hair and put on my makeup.

My hair was down to my midback and a scarlet red, curving in gentle waves. I'd inherited the shade from my father's side—he had been an immigrant from Scotland. My mother was a mixture of Scottish and Irish, and she was second-generation American. Both were magic-born, and my father had been a powerful witch—as powerful as my mother. I couldn't remember much about him, though. He had died when I was barely five, and my mother had raised me on her own. But Da had left me a trust fund, and my mother had never touched it, although she had worked several jobs to keep us afloat.

I poured boiling water over my instant oatmeal and then

flipped the switch on my espresso machine. It wasn't fancy, but it made good espresso and I was happy with it. I added some maple syrup to my porridge and set it on the table, then knelt to check on the egg.

It was brighter in color than it had been the night before, and I could still sense whatever was inside it was still alive. I returned to the kitchen and made myself a steaming hot vanilla latte, then sat down to eat breakfast.

After breakfast, I texted May: CAN YOU COME OVER TO TAKE A LOOK AT SOMETHING FOR ME? I FOUND IT IN THE MIDDLE OF THE NIGHT AND I NEED YOUR EXPERT OPINION. I'LL BE HOME UNTIL AROUND SIX, THEN I HAVE TO HEAD OUT FOR AN APPOINTMENT.

Before I could reach for my latte, she texted back, SURE. I'LL BE THERE AT AROUND TWO. SEE YOU THEN.

I checked on the egg again, then glanced outside. The clouds were starting to lift and I could feel the rain moving out for now. By afternoon, it would be warm and partially cloudy. It was still early—around eight-thirty. I decided that today, I'd tackle building the raised beds and planting my herb garden. They were in planters near my workshop, but I wanted to create my raised herb beds before the season was up to make certain they had acclimated.

The lumber for the beds was stained and weatherproofed, stacked in the utility shed. I wasn't an expert with a hammer and nails, but I figured I could manage a few squares on the ground. Then I'd fill the beds with soil and plant the herbs. To be honest, I had no real sense for how to efficiently build a raised bed, but it couldn't be rocket science.

I had planned it out on paper—four squares with walkways between each, and I had used string to mark out where the four beds would be. I wasn't clear on how to do it—but how hard could it be? Build a box without a bottom and fill it with soil. Easy, right?

After building the beds, I planned on paving the walkways between the containers with slate, like the sidewalks. The herb garden would be close to the house, as well as a raised bed for a kitchen garden. I wasn't sure what I wanted to plant —I wasn't a farmer, after all. But I wanted enough tomatoes to make growing a garden worth it, along with some greens, cucumbers, carrots, and if I was lucky, a couple pumpkins and watermelons.

I dragged the planks out of the utility shed, one by one, to the area where I was planning on building the beds. Then I brought out the toolbox and the hoe. As I began to dig a trench along the line of the string, I heard someone say, "Hello."

Turning, I saw a tall blond man crossing the line from the trailhead leading to May's house. He was fit, wearing a loose tank top, cargo shorts, and a pair of Birkenstocks. His hair flowed down to his shoulders, and he flashed me a good-natured smile.

I took off my gardening gloves and set down my hoe. "Hi. What can I do for you?"

"I'm Bran, May's son. I thought I'd come introduce myself since we haven't had the chance to meet yet."

I held out my hand and he shook it with a firm, dry grasp.

"I'm Elphyra. Your mother's been kind to me since I moved in." I motioned to the patio. "Would you like to sit down for a moment? Would you like some lemonade?"

He regarded me quietly for a moment, then nodded. "Thank you." As he followed me, he asked, "What are you doing? I mean, with the planks."

"I'm trying to build raised garden beds," I said. "I probably should have done more research, but I thought it was a no-brainer. Frame a box, fill with dirt, plant herbs. I worked in a plant nursery, but I took care of the plants and didn't have anything to do with the construction side of gardening."

"I hate to tell you this, but there's more to it than that," Bran said with a laugh. "I've built them for our farm and if you want good results, there are a number of steps that I think you're overlooking."

"Of course there are," I said with a grimace. "If I get the lemonade, can you fill me in on what I need to do?"

"You get the lemonade and I'll help you build your beds." He sat on one of the benches and leaned back, looking around. "You have a nice setup here. Cozy. I've always liked this cottage. I remember coming here for cookies and milk when Mrs. Jansen was alive. I would mow her lawn and help her with chores around the place."

I headed into the kitchen and found a tray, then added two glasses and a pitcher of lemonade. I peeked in the fridge and grabbed a package of pecan rolls. I put two of them on dessert plates, then carried the tray back to the patio. I set it on the picnic table and motioned for him to join me.

"I hope you don't think that I was hinting for help—I can do more research."

"Consider me research," Bran said, taking his place opposite of me at the table. "I'll show you how to do it, in case next time I'm not around."

I was stubborn, but gracious enough to accept help when it was offered. "Thank you. I'd appreciate that." I poured him some lemonade and handed him one of the rolls. "So, you're May's son. She said you mainly work on your farm. Have you always lived there?"

He nodded. "Yes, I was born there. I grew up in Starlight Hollow and have never felt the urge to move anywhere else. The town has evolved over the years, but the important parts have stayed the same. Good people, mostly. We have a tight-knit community that rallies together when necessary. And it's quiet here." He paused, then added, "My mother said you're from Port Townsend?"

I shrugged. "Yeah, I am. I had to get away, but I didn't want to put too much distance between my mother and me. She has my aunt and cousin, but otherwise, our family's scattered. My father died when I was young."

"I'm sorry. My father died five years ago. He was over near Humptulips, hunting for mushrooms. Unfortunately, it was also deer season and a drunk hunter saw him moving in the bushes and shot him dead. The hunter was sentenced to twenty-five years in prison without being eligible for parole. But I guarantee you, the day he's up for it, I'll be there asking them to deny it. Carrying around a rifle while you're belting back beers? Can you say 'stupid'?"

I stared at my glass. "I didn't know about that. May never mentioned it." It was a kick in the pants—reminding me that I wasn't the only one who had undergone tragedy. "How long were your parents married?"

"Let's see. Forty-six years, I think. I was born on their sixteenth anniversary—February twenty-seventh. My mother and father didn't think they were going to have children, then when she was forty, boom, I showed up. She jokes about me being their best-ever anniversary present."

"So, your mother is—"

"Seventy-three. She doesn't look it or act it, though." He saluted me with his glass. "Here's to the good memories. May they always outweigh the bad."

"She's active, all right." I tapped my glass against his. "Hear, hear."

After a moment, he sorted through my tools and materials. "Do you have black plastic to put down below to keep the weeds from sprouting up?"

I shook my head. "No, I didn't realize I needed it."

"You don't, technically, but it's going to help. I see you bought cedar planks for the sides?"

"Treated cedar," I said. "Is that right?"

"The best next if you're going with real wood. Do you have the soil yet?"

"No," I said. "I was going to get it all set up, then enlist the help of a friend to help me lug the soil back. I can fit it in my SUV, but those bags are *heavy*." I'd planned on roping Bree into helping. Shifters were always stronger than humans and magic-born, at least physically, and Bree liked physical activity more than I did. I was no slouch, but I wasn't the let's-rough-it-type.

"I'll have you set up by afternoon, since everything is pre-cut to size. Then we can buy your soil—and the plastic—tomorrow if you like. I can spare the morning to help. Let me finish my drink and then I'll take a look at what you have and see if you need any more supplies to start."

He polished off his lemonade and, carrying the last of the pecan roll, he headed toward the garden plot. Not sure what to do, I followed him after shutting the lid on the pitcher so bees or any other bugs wouldn't fly in.

I sat on the grass while he looked over the boards and the tools. The clouds continued to dissipate until the sky was bright blue, so bright that it almost hurt my eyes to look at it. A few white wisps of clouds drifted by as a light breeze sprang up. The wind was always blowing here, which I didn't mind.

"Do you have a rubber mallet?" Bran asked.

"I have no idea. The utility shed's over there and that's where all the outdoor tools are." I pointed to the shed. "It's unlocked."

He hiked over to the shed. As I watched him go, it occurred to me that Bran was handsome, in a rugged, Birken-stock sort of way. He didn't remind me of a witch at all, though May had mentioned he had psychic flashes, and a green thumb that wasn't normal. I usually didn't go for blonds but with his ready smile and easy nature, he reminded me of Rian in a way.

He returned, mallet in hand, along with a pickaxe and shovel. "This is a rubber mallet," he said. "Don't you know what tools you have in there?"

"I didn't stock the shed. I paid the contractor to buy a good array of tools the average homeowner might need and so...that's how I have what I have." I grinned at him. "I figured he would know what to buy better than me, so I left it up to the expert."

Bran chuckled. "Well, that's one way of doing it. Anyway, where are the corner posts for the beds?"

"Corner posts? I didn't know I needed them."

He restrained a sigh. "Corner posts will strengthen the bed, especially if you want to use it for more than one season. Do you... You know what? I'm going to go pick up a few things and I'll be back in an hour or so. You want anything else from town?"

"Let me give you the money for that—"

"I'll keep the receipts," he said, waving me off.

"All right. Why don't you pick up a pizza or sandwiches for our lunch and add that to the cost. I'd love a roast beef sub, butter and barbecue sauce—no mayo, no mustard. Lots of tomatoes, a leaf of lettuce."

"Text me. What's your number and I'll ping you so you can add me to your contacts."

I gave him my number and he texted me a smile emoji. I added him into my contacts. "Bran Anderson?"

"Right. Okay, text me what you want for lunch, and I'll stop at Simon's Subs on the way back." He waved, then jogged back toward the trailhead.

As I watched him retreat, I heard a noise from inside the house. Frowning, I darted in, following the noise. It was coming from near the woodstove. I crossed over to it and saw that the egg in the drawer was beginning to wobble. Frowning, I knelt beside it, and it was then that I saw that thin cracks were beginning to spread across the top of it.

Whatever was in that egg, was about to hatch.

CHAPTER SIX

"OH CRAP!" I HADN'T THOUGHT AHEAD AS TO WHAT TO DO
if the egg actually started to hatch. It had been too late at
night when I found it, and I'd been too tired to consider what
I was really doing. I set the dresser drawer on my bed and sat
down beside it, waiting. I didn't know if I should be helping
or not. Chickens broke out of their own eggs, so did ducks so
far as I knew. But this egg was a mystery—and if the internet
was right, it might be a dragonette—and I had no clue what
to do.

"Whatever you are, do you need help?" It was useless to
ask, but hearing the sound of my own voice calmed me down
a little. At that moment, my phone chose to ring and I
jumped, startled out of my thoughts. I glanced at the caller
ID. It was May. Relieved, I hit the speaker icon. "May, can
you come over now instead of waiting till two?"

"You sound frantic, girl. I was about to ask if Bran was
still there. He mentioned that he wanted to meet you this
morning." She sounded her usual matter-of-fact self.

"He is...or was. He went to buy corner posts for my raised

beds. May, can you please come over? I have a situation that I'm not sure how to deal with." I didn't want to sound frantic, but for some reason, I had a distinct sense that whatever was in that egg might need help. "I found something last night and I need your opinion on it. *Now.*"

"I'm on my way." She hung up.

I tossed my phone on the bed as I continued to watch the egg rock back and forth. As it wobbled, I leaned over the drawer. "If you can hear me, let me know if you want me to crack the shell for you." I paused, then muttered, "That's ridiculous. Whatever's in there isn't going to be able to understand me."

But at that moment, I distinctly heard a faint voice say, "Help."

"Help? Help who? Was that you? In the egg?" Feeling like I was caught up in some surreal joke, I hesitantly reached out to the egg and lightly ran my fingers over the spreading cracks. They were turning the egg into a mosaic, but they weren't deep enough to break open.

My nail file was thin enough to fit in the cracks. I jumped up and hurried over to my dresser, sifting through the containers I had spread across the top. One of the acrylic holders had the nail file, along with several emery boards. I grabbed the file and hurried back to the bed. Once there, I eyed the biggest crack and gently placed the tip of the file against it to see if the point would fit in the crack. It barely did. But if I applied pressure and it broke suddenly, then I ran the risk of stabbing whatever was inside.

"I don't know what to do!" I tried to tell myself that panicking was useless. After all, I had no clue what was in the egg. It could be a lizard. A snake, maybe. Well, not a snake. Snake eggs weren't that big and some snakes had live births, and I had no idea what the snakes around here did. I'd never thought to ask.

"Elphyra? Where are you?" May peeked around the bedroom door. "The door was unlocked."

"Hurray! You made good time."

"You sounded so frantic that I drove. What's the matter —" she paused, staring at the egg. "Oh good gods. You found a dragonette egg!"

"You're sure? I found it last night and now it's hatching and I heard it ask for help," I said, scooting over and dragging the box farther on the bed so she could sit on the other side. "How did you know what it is?"

May leaned down to examine it. "A long time ago, I was out hiking in the woods with Angus—my husband. I saw one then." She paused, then—catching my attention—said, "Slip the tip of that nail file into the side of the crack, not the top. Use it to gently add leverage to the side of the egg."

I did as she asked, while she gave me instructions on minor adjustments. The eggshell was cracking, and from inside, I could hear what sounded like scrabbling sounds. "Now what?"

"Now, break off the quarter-size piece that's hanging from that side."

I took hold of the shard and gingerly twisted it until it came off without breaking the rest of the egg. The next moment, there was a gasp from inside and a thin red-scaled arm, about the diameter of my thumb, reached out, ending in five "fingers" with long golden claws at their tips. I watched, mesmerized. Whatever it was, it had opposable thumbs.

"May—"

"Sshh. Wait." She reached into the drawer and turned the egg slightly. Why, I wasn't sure.

The next moment, another arm reached out. The hands clasped the edge of the hole in the shell and pushed from the inside. The shell cracked some more, and then a large chunk of the side fell away. I waited, breath bated.

Stepping out of the egg was a tiny red dragon, perfectly formed. Its wings were curled around its back and it slowly unfurled them, like a butterfly, before turning to me. As I met its gaze, everything else faded, everything but the dragonette.

Everything I thought I knew flew out the window. Dragons were massive creatures, seldom if ever seen, and they left humans alone. In fact, they had retreated to the highest reaches on the planet and lived between the worlds. But here in front of me, one had hatched, perfectly shaped, and the size of a small cat. A dragonette.

I held out my hand and it unsteadily stumbled toward me. With the other hand, I guided it onto my palm, barely touching it. Then, as it grasped my thumb with its tiny hands, I lifted the dragonette up to my face. We stared at each other, and for a moment, nothing else existed. I knew, absolutely knew, that we were meant to find each other and be together until the end.

"Who are you?" I whispered. "I'm Elphyra."

The dragonette stared at me and I tumbled into those beautiful blue eyes, falling hard. I wanted to protect the creature, to take care of it and guard it.

"Elphyra," it said, its voice lower than I would have thought possible for such a tiny creature. The next moment, I felt the dragonette's presence in my mind, searching. It didn't feel like it was intruding—*he* was learning. And as sure as I knew who I was, I knew this dragonette was male. And though he had just hatched, he was far older in spirit than most of the people I'd ever met during life. Apparently they matured while in the egg and emerged fully aware.

A flood of images cascaded through my mind. He was a dragonette, and he had no idea where his mother was. And he was small, but he'd grow bigger through the centuries. He wouldn't be full grown by the time I left this planet, though.

I'd never see him fully grown because his kind were few and far between, and they lived long lives. But the bond was there between us, an unbreakable cord connecting us. He'd chosen *me*, and we'd be bound forever, unless one of us died. Then, and only then, would the bond break.

"You *know* me," I said, gazing into his eyes. "You know who I am." I had no idea how, but this creature was a part of me. I brought him close to my chest and the dragonette snuggled in, under my chin. I felt a rumble almost like a purr and glanced over at May.

"What's going on?" I asked.

"Bonding. He's sealing the bonding process." Her eyes were luminous, and she reached out, not touching the wings, but hovering near. The dragonette looked like he was asleep. I wasn't sure what to do next.

"Have you ever seen one before?" I asked.

"A couple, but they're. Their mothers lay the larva and tends to them. Then, after a time, the larva spin their eggs around them. At that time, the mother scatters them in different places. It's theorized that she's hoping at least one will survive and not become some coyote's dinner. If there's somebody nearby with compatible energy, as the dragonette nears its time to hatch, it will automatically reach out from within the egg and touch their minds, trying to lead them to the egg."

"What does he eat? What's he going to want? I've had cats before and I miss them, but I have no clue what to feed him, or how to take care of him." I paused, then asked, "How long do they live? Do they always bond with people? How big will he get?"

"First, he can eat whatever he wants. He needs meat, but dragonettes aren't obligate carnivores. Second, as to taking care of him, well...for the most part they look after themselves. There are a few rare vets who understand their anatomy, but annual vet visits are few and far between."

I looked over at her. "You know people who are bonded, don't you?"

May let the question settle for a moment. "You might say so. What few researchers there are on them tend to keep information on how to find the eggs to themselves, because the danger of poaching is very real. There are millionaires who would pay a high price to own one of these, but if they snatch a dragonette that's hatched and bonded and try to force it to re-bond, it would be torture for both the dragonette and their witch. And in the end, it wouldn't work. So most people who have dragonettes don't advertise the fact. They keep the knowledge private, telling a select few about it —people they can trust."

Sobering, I began to see the drawbacks. "So I should create a secret room for him?"

"No, that's not necessary. Dragonettes—like their massive cousins—have the ability to phase into another dimension. It's not the astral realm, but one that only a few species can enter. Unicorns, pegasi, sphinxes, Nessie and her cousins, can phase in and out of our world when they need to. Some live mostly in this secret realm. Those who research cryptozoology call the realm *Sescernaht*—the secret night." She smiled. "So if he needs to, he'll be able to vanish. They can travel through that realm, which means he can phase into Sescernaht here, then travel a ways there and appear someplace else in our realm. Dragonettes have an innate sense of direction and they're good with spatial relationships."

"You certainly know your lore on them," I said. Inwardly, though, I was worried. I didn't know if I was up to the responsibility of taking care of the baby dragon. Hell, I wasn't sure I could take care of *myself*.

May must have sensed my hesitation, because she added, "You don't have a choice, Elphyra. He's chosen you and the bonding process has taken place. The only thing that will shatter it is the death of either the dragonette or their person."

"What will happen to him when I die?" I hated to think of the pain that might cause.

"Then he'll strike out on his own. Not all dragonettes bond with people—they're a solitary, isolated species. But once bound, they will never transfer their connection to another. And when that connection comes to an end, they revert to their solitary state." She leaned in to look at him. He was curled asleep in my arms, next to my chest. "He'll sleep for a few hours. You can lay him down. The connection has formed."

"Okay, out with it. How do you know so much about them?" I asked, settling him onto the blanket next to the shards of the broken egg.

May inhaled a sharp breath. "Truth? Few people know, but I was once bound to a green dragonette. Her name was Melda. She was born with a birth defect, though, and she died when I was in my fifties. She was with me for about ten years, but I can tell you, I felt like my heart had been ripped out when she died. She died in my arms, and I did my best to make her comfortable until the end. I can't tell you how much it hurt—and it still hurts, but time has softened the loss. I survived and I'm the better for having known her."

Yet another secret about May that served to deepen the way I thought of her. "Do you think Melda's mother stuck around the area and laid this egg?"

"It's possible, I suppose, though I doubt it. Now, usually, the mother gives birth to babies who match her coloration," May said. "You'll need to think of a name for him. He'll be able to talk—they're born with the ability to immediately understand the language their bond-partner speaks. It's automatic and is the result of the process of bonding." She helped me adjust the blanket so that the dragonette was covered, yet not too warm.

At that moment, Bran's voice echoed from the front door. "Anybody home? I brought lunch."

"We're back here, Bran," May called out. "In the bedroom!"

"Should I tell him about the dragonette?" I asked.

"You can tell him," she said to me. "He was fifteen when Melda died, but he remembers her and he'll never breathe a word."

A moment later, Bran peeked through the door. "Hey, Ma —what..." He stared at the dragonette. "That's..."

"Yeah," I said. "I found the egg out in the woods last night. It was calling to me and I went out tramping through the thicket at two A.M."

Bran knelt on one knee next to May, peering into the dresser drawer. "Do you think there's any family connection to—" he paused, glancing at his mother.

"Melda? I doubt it. Although given how long dragonettes live, it's possible."

He smiled, and I realized at that moment, how genuinely handsome he was—and the smile reinforced his good looks. And...he felt safe. Safe in a way that I wasn't used to.

"Well, I'm going to get to work on those beds for you. Don't worry about helping. You have your hands full as it is."

As he ducked out of the bedroom, I let out a sigh. "Okay, so I need a name for him. And food. Ground meat to start? Or does he have teeth?"

"He has sharp needle teeth and fangs like a kitten. He can eat ground meat easily, both raw and cooked. Dragonettes have cast-iron stomachs. He can also eat bread, soft fruits and vegetables—no carrots or potatoes unless cooked. He'll tell you his preferences, probably by spitting out what he doesn't like." She laughed. "My Melda was brand-sensitive. There was one type of squash she loved, one type of meat, but she'd eat *all* the crappy cereals if I let her—she had a sweet tooth. But sugar's not good for anybody, dragonettes included."

I rolled my eyes. "I don't make it a huge part of my diet."

"I wouldn't want to be around a dragonette hyped up on sugar. Especially since most of them can spit jets of fire when they get agitated." She motioned for me to follow her and we left him sleeping in the dresser drawer as we headed into the living room. Both a sub sandwich and a pizza waited on the counter.

"I need to meet a woman named Darla tonight around six, along with her daughter Georgie. They have a haunted house problem and asked me to check on it for them. Would you be willing to…" I was about to ask May if she could babysit, though that sounded ridiculous. But she picked up on my question without me finishing.

"Will I watch over him? Of course. Do you have food for him?"

I thought about what I had in my fridge. Half a dozen eggs, some tomatoes, and a bowl of two-day-old tuna salad. "Nope, that's not going to do." A glance in the cupboards told me that they weren't any more helpful. "Is there a super-market near here? If you have time to stay with him now, I can go buy groceries so he'll have food when he wakes up."

"Try Bayside Market—it's new, and not far from here. I'll text you the directions. But *you* need to eat something first." May patted my hand. "Don't worry, you'll get along with him. It's your responsibility to think of a name for him. They all have their secret names, but you're the one who'll give him a name for this world."

"I'll be back soon! Thanks!" I grabbed my purse and keys,

then—sub sandwich in hand—I dashed out the door and made a beeline for my car. Fitting the key into the ignition, bite of sandwich between my teeth, I backed out of my driveway as May's text with the directions to the store came through. My life had changed drastically in the last twelve hours, and I wasn't sure what to think about it.

CHAPTER SEVEN

BAYVIEW MARKET WAS ABOUT A MILE AWAY FROM MY house, tucked between a vet's office called Dr. Carly's Cat Hospital and a pot shop called Hi Jinx. I thought about it for a moment and decided it was brilliant marketing for the grocery store to open next to a pot shop. It probably helped both.

My mind still whirling from the events of the day, I grabbed a shopping cart from outside the market doors and hurried inside. The automatic doors opened onto the produce section, which had an amazing array of bright-colored vegetables. The market was busy—afternoon seemed a popular time to buy groceries.

I dropped some veggies and fruit into the cart, then added eggs and butter and a half gallon of milk. A couple loaves of bread—I preferred French so I bought two long baguettes—and then, a loaf of sandwich bread for toast. At the meat aisle I selected hamburger and ground pork, sausage, a couple steaks, a small roast, and then various lunch meats into the cart.

"I wonder if he'd like cat food," I muttered, adding a

variety box of seafood-flavored cans to my growing pile. If he didn't like it, I'd give it to May. She had several cats.

Coffee was a must as well, and chips and a package of sandwich cookies. Tampons and toilet paper were also on the list, and as I spied the baby food, it occurred to me that might work if the dragonette's stomach was upset.

I have to think of a name for him, I thought, but my mind was blank. I'd have to feel out his personality first. After paying for my groceries, I stopped at the espresso stand in the store and ordered an iced double-caramel mocha. I was heading out the automatic doors, fishing in my purse for my keys, when I rammed right into a cart entering the store.

Sighing, I started to apologize and found myself staring into the eyes of Faron Collinsworth.

CRAP, I thought. Not again. Was I going to literally run into this guy *every time* we came into close proximity? Our cart wheels had locked together. I rattled my cart, trying to pull it back, but all I managed was to yank his forward.

"Would you *stop* doing that? You're making things worse," he said, shooting me a look of contempt. It would have withered me, *if* I cared about his opinion.

"Then *you* untangle them," I said. Not the apology I had planned on, but right now I wasn't feeling altogether apologetic.

"I will, if you'd hold your cart still," he countered.

Simultaneously, I gave one last yank, and his cart wheel rolled over his foot.

"Damn it!" He snarled, "For the love of all that's holy, let go of your cart and I'll separate them."

Frowning—I didn't like being talked to like that, but considering that I had just, perhaps, broken his toe, I figured he had the right to be miffed. I backed away, holding my coffee and purse. He bent down, his broad shoulders catching my attention. I didn't like him, but I had to admit, the wolf shifter was built. He puttered with the wheels for a moment, then, still scowling, he stood.

"I'm not sure how this happened, but I can't pry them apart. Go get another cart and we'll transfer your bags to it. It's going to take a wrench to wedge these apart." Hands on his hips, he kicked his cart.

"Hey, knock it off. Violence isn't the answer." I glanced around and saw a couple spare carts near the doors. "Here," I said, retrieving them. "One for you, one for me. I'll transfer my groceries. You can be on your way."

"I'll help," he said, stepping in to grab a bag of my groceries. Once again, I managed to step right in his way and he put his hand on my shoulder to push me back. I shook him off and he snorted. "Good gods, chill out. I'm not making a pass."

"Chill out? You're telling *me* to *chill out?*" Something about his attitude and abrupt nature pissed the hell out of me. "You're the one who sounds like you're about ready to punch somebody. I told you, I can do this. Go buy your Alpo or whatever it is you wolf shifters eat."

That touched a nerve. "*What* did you say to me?" He took a deep breath, a shocked look on his face, as though I'd slapped him.

I took advantage of the moment to start transferring the bags into the new cart. He placed the bag into my cart, still silent. I realized that my slur had hit him harder than if I'd punched him in the nose. I set the last bag in my cart and took a deep sigh.

"Listen," I said. "I took things a step too far. I apologize for that last crack. I guess the old saying is true, put a witch and a wolf shifter together and all you'll end up with is trouble. I'm truly sorry."

Faron tilted his head, holding my gaze. His scowl softened and, after a moment, he spoke. "Apology accepted. I shouldn't have called you 'witch' in that tone." He paused, then added, "Listen...I know this is an abrupt change of topic, but by any chance would you have time to talk to me for a moment? I'm in need of an expert opinion on something that might be magical in nature."

"And you want my advice?" I raised an eyebrow. "You sure you want to consult a *witch*?"

He sighed. "Again, I'm sorry. And trust me, given we've now butted heads twice, I'd rather ask *anybody* else. But you might be able to help and I don't know many other witches— not ones I trust. With your mouth, I figure you'll tell me the truth, no matter what I want to hear."

I snorted and finally smiled. "Well, I suppose I'll take that as a compliment, and yes, I don't give *rah-rah-go-team-go* advice when the truth is anything but that."

Glancing at the groceries, I tried to sort out my thoughts. I didn't want to talk to Faron, and yet—if I were being honest, he intrigued me. But today wasn't the day. I needed to get home because of the dragonette, and I had the meeting with Darla coming up.

"Not today, I'm sorry. But I can meet you tomorrow...or rather, if you come out to my place, we can talk." I wasn't sure how soon it would be before the dragonette would be able to stay by himself. I'd have to ask May when I arrived home.

After an uncertain pause, Faron finally said, "All right. Will noon work? I can get an hour or so off of work."

I nodded. "Noon will work. Do you know where I live?"

"Out on the old Jansen land." He paused, then hesitantly asked, "Are you going to be all right out there?"

It seemed like an odd question. "I haven't had any trouble yet. Why?"

"No reason," he said. "I thought I'd ask. I'll see you tomorrow at noon." He stood back so I could get through the door, then began talking to the bag boy who had arrived to see what the fuss about the carts was.

As I drove home, I wondered what Faron Collinsworth could want with my advice. And why had he asked if everything was okay on my land?

BRAN HAD FINISHED BUILDING the beds for the herb garden by the time I arrived home. Surprised by how quickly he had worked, I walked over to examine them. They were far better than anything I could have built.

Each of the four beds rested three feet above the ground, making for easy upkeep. My back would be thanking him for as long as I used them. The wood was treated cedar, like I had originally planned, but the resemblance ceased at that point. The corner pieces were decorative as well as functional, the beds were filled with dirt up to two inches below the top, and it had been tamped down to make sure it wouldn't sink too far when I watered it.

"I can put in that slate walkway for you tomorrow, if you'd like," Bran said. He was standing there, bare chested, sweat glistening on his skin. He wasn't ripped like a bodybuilder, but the man had muscle and a six-pack and I found my gaze lingering a little too long.

"Thank you. I don't know what to say." I ran my hand along one of the cedar planks, wondering if Bran's skin was as smooth as it looked. Yanking my thoughts away from what felt like dangerous territory, I added, "This was so much work—"

"Not really. Everything was ready to assemble, and I'm good with my hands."

"I bet you are," I murmured.

"What did you say?" He gave me a long look and I blushed and turned my head.

"Nothing...just that..." I backtracked. "Yes, you are good with your hands. This is lovely craftsmanship." I paused, glancing back at the car. "I'm sorry, I need to get the groceries—"

"I'll do it. You go in and talk to my mother." He picked up his shirt and slid it over his head.

I looked away, confused. It had been so long since I had last noticed any man other than Rian in any way remotely sexual that the feelings took me by surprise. Flustered and not sure what to think, I thanked him again and headed inside.

May was waiting in the kitchen.

"Your son is a genius with wood. Did you see the garden beds he built for my herb garden?"

She nodded. "I did. He loves to help out when he can. I raised him to believe in the good of helping others, as long as they don't take advantage of you."

"Well, I'm more than willing to pay for his time," I said. "I could never have constructed anything that nice." I looked around. "Is it—*he*—still asleep?"

At that moment, in answer to my question, the drag-onette flew out, as graceful as could be, and landed on my shoulder. I tried not to jump at his touch but a tingle of excitement raced through me. I found myself happy to see him, in fact—I was relieved to see him.

"Well, I guess that answers that," I said.

"You're back." In perfect English, with a faint British accent, the dragonette went on to add, "I presume you have a name for me?"

I blinked. The formality of the question startled me, as well as the perfect English. "You want me to name you *now*?"

"I'd appreciate it if you did," he said, sounding oddly like Giles French, an English butler—a character I remembered from a show I watched in re-runs when I was a little girl. He snorted and tiny puffs of steam—or was it smoke?—came out of his nostrils.

I glanced at May. "Well, then..." I tried to think but the sight of the smoke captivated me. I shook my head. "Don't torch anything, please."

"I'm not going to burn your house down!" The drag-onette's eyes swirled, and he fluttered his wings. "I may be freshly hatched but I'm capable of controlling the sparks."

I opened my mouth, then closed it again. So this was the way things were going to be. Of course, I'd end up with a snarky one. "Was Melda like this?"

May laughed. "No, though she was spunky."

"Not so *what*, might I ask?" The dragonette cleared his throat, sounding offended.

"Don't get bent," I said, laughing. "Well, Fancypants, you have a name now."

The dragonette stared at me. "You're naming me *Fancypants*?"

"Yeah, I am. And trust me, it fits." I stuck my tongue out at the dragonette.

He rolled his eyes, puffing smoke in my face. "I guess that will do."

"Heaven help the both of you," May said, snickering. She wiped her eyes. "The pair of you belong together. I can't wait to see how this all plays out."

"I'm hungry," Fancypants said. "You're my person. *Feed me*."

"Geez, entitled much?" I stared at him. How the hell was this going to work out?

At that moment, Bran came in, carrying four of the grocery bags. "Two left, I'll get them now." He started at the dragonette. "Did you find a name yet?"

May snorted. "Yes, yes she did."

"I named you 'Fancypants,' and 'Fancypants' you shall be," I said, starting to put the groceries away. "I'll fix you lunch in a moment."

Bran let out a laugh, then headed back out for the rest of the bags. As I finished the third bag, Bran returned with the last two. I tucked everything away in the fridge and cupboards, then took out some ground beef. "Fancypants, do you want your meat cooked or raw?"

"Either way." He flew over to the counter and hovered above where I was working. "I'm not partial to either—at least not yet. But I do require food. You have no idea how taxing it is to hatch out of an egg."

"Well, you've got me there. I definitely don't have a clue about that. So, how much do you want?" I pointed to the pound of ground beef in front of me.

"Half of that, please," he said, his eyes spiraling. They were mesmerizing—like white and blue pinwheels spinning in the wind.

At least he was polite, I thought as I placed half of the meat on a plate and set it on the counter. He dove into it, his neck twisting and bobbing like a snake's. As he devoured the meal, I wondered again what I had gotten myself into.

After a moment, another thought struck me. "Is being bonded to a dragonette like having a familiar?"

May thought about it for a moment, then nodded. "Somewhat. Though it's a different form of connection, not necessarily based on the magic."

I motioned for her to follow me into the living room while Fancypants was eating. Bran joined us. I sat in the rocking chair, while May sat on the sofa and Bran, an ottoman. I opened a window to let in the fresh air, and stared out into the yard. The flowers along the walkway looked beautiful, and I could see the herb garden beds from where I stood. My home was cozy and getting cozier, and I intended on keeping it that way.

"What happens if I want to get a cat or a dog? Will Fancypants attack them? Are dragonettes territorial?" It occurred to me that there was so much about this that I didn't know, and I'd better learn damned fast. I turned back to May.

"They *are* territorial, but primarily around others of their kind," she answered. "No one has ever successfully bonded with two at one time, as far as I know. As for other pets, I think you'd be safe. You might have to lay down some ground rules, but once bonded, the dragonette has to abide by your wishes—at least to some degree. It's not like a djinn. They aren't bound to serve you in whatever you wish, regardless of how you treat them. Mistreat them, and they will fight back. But the witch is generally the one in control."

I thought about Fancypants. Although he wasn't turning out to be quite what I expected—I didn't know *what* I expected—I felt the connection. "*Can* someone who's bonded to one mistreat them? I can't imagine that."

"Most people who are bonded couldn't bring themselves to hurt their dragonette, not deliberately. The bond is too strong. But there are dark hearts in the world, as you well know, and as I mentioned, there are nefarious people who are so rich and powerful that they'll pay a bounty hunter to find a dragonette egg. They try to force the bonding, but all it does is kill the dragonette. They are innately good creatures, and they cannot work with those who intend evil."

I started to say something, but May held her finger to her lips as Fancypants came flying in. He landed on the coffee table and gave a delicate burp. Wisps of smoke flared from his nostrils. It was so freaking cute that I had to force myself not to laugh.

"Did you get enough to eat?" I asked. "Do you want anything else?"

"I'm good," he said, bobbing his head as he let out a wide yawn. "Now, I must sleep." And with that, he promptly curled up on a throw pillow and began to snore.

"That was quick," I said.

"He'll be out for hours," May said. "For the first couple of months, after they eat they sleep long and hard as they get adjusted to life outside the egg. The naps will eventually grow shorter. You should find a good bed for him where he won't be interrupted and where he won't be in the way while he sleeps."

"You think he'd like a dog bed?" I asked.

"A cushy cat bed would be better, or a cat tree—drag-onettes like to be up high."

"I feel like I adopted a flying cat who can talk," I said. "Same attitude, same preferences."

"Dragonettes get along well with cats. They understand each other," May said. She turned to Bran. "Do you remember Melda?"

"Some," he said. "She spied on me and told you when I wasn't doing my homework. She also liked to steal your jewelry."

"Oh, yes—I remember that," May said. "That's another thing to watch for. They're like crows in that they're attracted to shiny things. You might want to get Fancypants his own treasure box and give him trinkets now and then. That might prevent him from going for your jewelry and keys and what-ever else catches his fancy."

This was beginning to rack up the expenses. "Does it have to be real gold?"

"No, gold plate, silver, shiny jeweled glass...even aluminum will work, as long as it sparkles. If he were a full-sized dragon? You'd better hand over the real goods, but dragonettes aren't as picky."

Bran glanced at his watch. "I have to leave. I have a grange meeting in an hour or so. We're discussing the upcoming Summer Shoreside Festival."

"What's that?" I asked.

"A street festival down by the farmers market that happens every July. It's like the market on steroids, with artists joining in, and a couple of concerts, and some of the restaurants vend as well. There are competitions for the best preserves, pickles, and so on. Like an upscale country fair. The grange sponsors it and since I belong to the grange, I need to be there." He kissed May on the cheek. "I'll be home for dinner."

"I'll be over here, watching Fancypants," she said. "I'll leave you something to heat up." She patted his cheek. Their connection was tangible, but although Bran obviously loved his mother, he wasn't a mama's boy and May seemed happy to let him lead his own life.

As he left, I glanced at my phone. It was four o'clock. "I didn't mean to take up your entire day," I said. "I'm sorry."

"Not a problem," May said. "But I'll get myself home now, and make dinner for Bran. I'll be back by five-thirty. Will that be enough time for you to make your appointment?"

"Plenty. I don't have to be at Darla's until seven. Thanks again, for everything."

As I saw her out, I glanced at the sky. The evening promised to be clear, but I could smell clouds on the horizon —they smelled like thunder and lightning, and set a restless edge in my aura. I thought about planting the herbs, but a voice inside told me maybe I should spend some time in meditation before heading over to Darla's.

CHAPTER EIGHT

DARLA LIVED ON ROXBERRY STREET, AND AS I PULLED UP to the house at precisely seven P.M., I saw Bree was already there. She had texted me when I was on the way over saying she planned to be there as well, in case there was any awkwardness. I read between the lines though. Bree was here because she was worried Kevin might have changed his mind on the bowling. Bree had been in an abusive relationship in her early twenties and now she did her best to run interference in what could be tricky situations.

I parked next to her car and stepped out, leaning on the open door as I examined the house from a distance. It was two stories, Craftsman style by the look of it, and it hadn't weathered the years well. The paint on the wooden siding was peeling off, and in one section, it looked like someone had started scraping it clean. There were seven steps leading up to a porch that spanned the front of the house. Beyond the knee wall, there was a large bay window to the right, and to the left, a smaller window.

Above the first story, a single window looked out from the center of the house. The curtain covering it was sheer, but as

I watched, something pulled it back and two gleaming eyes stared down at me. Startled, I stared back. They burned brilliant crimson, then faded away. Whatever that was, it wasn't human. Shivering, I walked up the sidewalk, toward the porch.

Bree peeked out the screen door, motioning for me to come in. "We're in luck. Kevin's out for now." She wrapped her arm through mine. "This place is creepy as hell."

"It feels it. Even when I was in my car, I could sense something here, and I thought I saw someone—or *thing*—watching me from the upstairs window a moment ago."

As we approached the door, a feeling of dread swept over me. I drew closer to Bree. "Can you sense it?" I stopped, sniffing the air. "I smell something here—it's like...rotten eggs or decaying meat. I don't like this." I was rapidly changing my mind about helping, but then I saw Darla, her face hopeful, and I knew that I wasn't going to walk away. At least, not yet.

I glanced around the room. We were in a small foyer, and to the left of me was a staircase, heading up to the second floor, flush with the outside wall. It made a sharp turn back on itself a third of the way up. From where I was standing, I couldn't see where it led. Beneath the upper part of the stairwell was a small storage space, with a few boxes sitting in it.

Ahead, the foyer led to a dining room, and to the right was an archway leading into the living room. Farther along the right wall—once we were in the dining room—was a set of French doors, also leading into the living room.

"Well, I can tell you right now, if I hadn't promised to check things out, I would turn around and get the hell out of this place," I said. The house felt like one big black hole, ready to swallow us and not let go.

"It's making me want to shift into my puma self," Bree said. "Everything feels prickly, like when you get entangled in a briar patch." As we entered the dining room, she said, "Elphyra is here."

Darla was sitting at the table, along with Georgie. "Thank you for coming. I sent Mary and John off to their friends for the evening. For one thing, I don't want them telling Kevin about this, and second, I don't want them here in case your presence stirs anything up."

"Good thinking," I said, looking around. There were two doors against the back wall of the dining room—one closed, and the other an archway leading to the kitchen. The dining room had one other door, on the back right of the room. "Why don't you show me around first? I'd rather do that before we get into specifics, so I can form an unbiased opinion."

I didn't tell her that my opinion was already biased, but I also didn't want what she had to say to cloud over what information I might get on my own.

"Why don't we start here, then. This is obviously the dining room," she said. "Tell me when you want to move on to another room."

I wandered around, occasionally touching a picture here or there. There was an oriel window—three sided—with a window seat beneath it, overlooking the side yard. The green drapes on the two outer windows were held back by gold swag ropes, and the center window had a sheer valance over the top, and a set of vertical blinds that were open. The floor was tiled, and the walls were pale gold. A dark wood table sat in front of the closed door to the back, and a matching china hutch sat against the wall that divided the room from the foyer. The hutch was oddly empty and I wondered if they had neglected to unpack or if there was another reason.

As I walked around the room, approaching the closed door behind the table, I shivered. As I reached out to touch the knob, the metal sparked against my fingers with a nasty shock and I jerked my hand back.

"Crap, that stung." I turned around. "What's behind this door?"

"The basement," Darla said.

"It's creepy as fuck," Georgie added. "Mary and Johnny won't go down there, and I don't blame them. The basement's not finished. Two sides of it are cement blocks part way, then rammed dirt the rest of the way up. It's filled with a bunch of old junk that was here when we moved in."

I glanced at Darla. "What kind of junk?"

"Chests, boxes full of what looks like radio crap, magazines—I don't know. And below the staircase there are shelves and some jars that look like they were used for canning. A few are still full and I expect they're so old the food would kill you if you ate the contents."

"Well, something went on down there and whatever it was, it was bad. I'll check it out after we go through the main house." I glanced at Bree and gave a small shake of my head and she nodded back.

Darla led us into the kitchen. A galley kitchen, the sink and dishwasher were on the left, and the refrigerator and counterspace were on the other side. A closed door nestled between the fridge and the counter.

"That's the bathroom," Darla said. "And through here," she led us to the back of the kitchen, "we have the back porch...mudroom...whatever you want to call it."

I peeked into the mudroom. Long and narrow, it contained a chest freezer and a washer and dryer, along with a rack for hanging clothes. A bench sat opposite the freezer, where you could sit to take off your shoes. A door flush against the back of the house led to the backyard.

I peeked out to see a double lot. Part of the yard had been rototilled for what looked like an extensive garden. A few fruit trees were scattered along the fence to the right, and to the left a hedge provided privacy from the neighbors. Even from where I stood, I could feel a tainted blight that underscored the house and land that it stood on.

"Let's move on," I said, turning to follow Darla.

She and Georgie led us back through the kitchen, into the bathroom. The room was small, crowded, and gave me the creeps. A second door near the wash basin led into the master bedroom. We had made a loop, and were behind the closed door leading into the dining room.

The master bedroom had a big bed, a dresser, a compact stationary bike in one corner, and a closet, but the room felt tainted in the same way as the backyard.

"Okay, living room next and then if you'll show us the upstairs," I said.

"Are you sensing anything?" Georgie asked.

"More than I want to," I said.

Darla led us back into the dining room, then we made a quick sweep through the living room, which—so far—felt like the most neutral room in the house. After that, we headed upstairs.

As we swung around the landing where the steps turned back on themselves, I could see a door at the top of the stairs, and a hallway leading to the left. I wanted nothing to do with either. My blood chilled as we neared the end and I held my breath as we passed by the hall. As Darla opened the door directly in front of us, I tried to ignore the hallway to our left because I knew—*I just knew*—that there'd be something there, looking back.

"This is Mary and Georgie's room," Darla said, as we entered.

The room was standard size, though it had an odd ceiling that was slanted all along the right side. Anybody too tall would have trouble walking along the back side of the room.

There were two closets—one a door to the left that was closed with a lock was on it, bolted shut, and then an archway to the right that had a beaded curtain across it.

There were two single beds, one large dresser with two columns of drawers, a desk against one corner with schoolbooks on it, two nightstands, and somehow they had also managed to find room for a toy box near one of the beds.

The walls were painted a soft rose, with leaf-green trim. Sage curtains covered the window. I realized that this was the window through which someone had been staring at me when I first arrived. I glanced around, waiting for whoever it was to show themselves, but they decided to lurk in the shadows, unwilling to make themselves known.

"All right, any other questions?"

"What about Mary? Is she a target, too?" Bree asked.

"Several times over the past few weeks, she's come down the stairs, asking if we were calling her. Neither Kevin nor I had said anything. She also told me that she keeps seeing a dark shadow in the corner of this room."

"I've seen it too," Georgie said, leading the way over to the corner with the desk in it. She pointed to the wall. "One night while I was trying to meditate—Mary was downstairs— I smelled something odd. When I opened my eyes, I looked over in that corner of the ceiling and I saw a dark cloud hovering there. It smelled like rancid meat, and when as I stood up, it vanished."

"What did you feel when you saw it?"

"Terrified. Whatever it is, it's *not* friendly. It hovered there, swirling, for a moment, then disappeared." Georgie shivered.

"Why do you have a lock on the closet door?" I asked, examining the deadbolt.

"Mary hates this closet, so I use it." Georgie pulled the bolt back and opened the closet door. Inside, against one wall, was a two-foot-square patch against the wall. It was on a hinge and opened to the side. "That provides access to a second attic space. And that's why we keep the closet door locked. That panel keeps opening on its own, and the closet door did too, before we put the deadbolt on it."

I walked into the closet and stopped as the panel creaked open by itself. "Okay, then," I said, turning around and walking right out.

"Are you going to ask who's here?" Darla asked.

"No," Bree spoke up, her eyes wide. "Whatever's in this house—and though I'm not psychic, I can feel how powerful the entities are here—is awake and listening to us."

"She's right. I'll wait until I've seen the whole house," I said, trying to act nonchalant, though I wanted to turn tail and run. Even dealing with a vampire was better than this. "Okay, why don't you show me the back room. I take it that's the last?"

"There's a small hall bathroom and the attic crawlspace, but otherwise yes, that's it." Darla led the way back to the stairs. We had to go down two steps to walk up the two side steps leading into the hallway.

The moment we stepped into the hall, a sinking feeling spread through my stomach. Besides the basement, this hall was strong with the spreading shadow that crept through the house. There were two pocket doors to the left, and a door at the end.

"Where do those lead?" I asked.

"The first is the powder room I mentioned, and the second leads to an attic space—separate from the one in Georgie's closet. The room at the end is Johnny's room." Darla shivered. "We have problems getting Johnny to go to bed. He cries every night before we can finally get him to come up to his room."

"Johnny's sensitive. I think he has the makings of a medium," Georgie said.

"Right," said Darla. "Several times, I'll wake up and find him asleep on the sofa in the living room. He says that the 'two old ladies' in the attic won't let him sleep. When I ask him about it, he says they scold and pinch him when he's in bed." Her face paled. "The other night he told me that one of them said he belongs with them, and that he's going to be with them forever. And now, Kevin's starting to yell at him, calling him a baby. I put a stop to it, but..."

Darla opened the door to Johnny's room and I felt flattened by the energy rushing out of it, as though we'd opened the door to a wind tunnel.

"Holy crap," I said, motioning for her to move to the side as I stepped into the room. The room had an odd shape, with a slanted ceiling on one side like Georgie and Mary's room, and a large column stood in the center of the room. *Load-bearing*, I thought.

There was no door on the closet, nor secret passage inside, but the energy was dank. Dank and dangerous. As I stuck my head inside, I thought I could hear someone saying *Come here—we have candy and toys for you.* Jumping back, I turned to the others.

"Did you hear that?"

They shook their heads, though Bree gave me a look asking what the hell was up.

"Your son, Johnny—you say he's sensitive? Psychic?"

Darla hesitated, then nodded. "I think he is. I've noticed it before, that he can pick up on things I'm thinking, or he'll know something he's not supposed to know. And once he told me that his grandma came to visit. She's been dead since before he was born, but he described her perfectly."

"Then you need to keep him out of this room—off this floor

entirely," I said. I circled the room and at one point, I paused, thinking I saw a shadow cross the opposite wall where there shouldn't be any shadows. "Show me the attic space, please."

We moved back into the hall and I stood stock still, staring at the pocket door that opened into the attic. I had no desire to face whatever was in there, but Darla and her family needed help and I could probably make things better, at least to some degree.

As long as it isn't a vampire, I thought, reaching out to open the door. Another shock resonated through my fingers. "All right, stand back." I motioned for them to all get out of the hall and onto the steps, then opened the door and stepped in. Immediately, a massive force tried to blast me out. Two old women were sitting there, in rocking chairs, wearing high-necked, ankle-length dresses. Their eyes blazed as they continued their assault.

Before I could stop myself I blurted out, "Holy fuck, knock it off, you two!"

The women froze, looking straight at me as though they hadn't expected me to *talk* to them. The taller one—she had brownish-gray hair in a messy bun on the top of her head, and she was wearing a dress consistent with the early 1920s— stood, an indignant look on her face.

Her partner—sister—whatever they were to each other— was petite and so prim and proper that she made my head hurt. She wore a long black dress with a high neck and she had a silver bun atop her head, perfectly coiffed. They radiated so much hatred that I couldn't get a good read on them other than their chaotic anger.

I brought up a barrier between them and me, drawing on the energy of the smoky quartz of my pendant. Their fury died down and I was able to examine them closer without the blinding rage that they were sending my way. I managed to get in a moment or two of observation before they realized I wasn't being affected by their attack.

They were ghosts, all right, but more than ghosts. There was an odd corporeal quality to them that my mind went to zombies, but I didn't know if zombies actually existed. They weren't vampires, I knew that much. No, they were spirits but...

The one with the silver hair stood. She was clutching something in her hand and I strained, trying to see what it was. The brunt of the power was coming from whatever it was.

"Bree," I said, motioning her over. Puma shifters had heightened eyesight. "What's she holding—there, in her left hand?"

"Needles—it looks like knitting needles and some sort of item that she's knitting. There's something on one of those needles." Bree glanced at me. "That's her anchor."

"And I'll bet that there's a chest in the basement containing those needles and whatever she was knitting. We need to find them." I turned to Darla. "We need to go down to the basement."

"Won't they try to stop us?" she asked, fear crossing her face.

"I don't know. I can't keep this barrier up while also searching for the anchor that keeps them tethered here, but if they attack us, I'll do everything I can to stop them." I turned to Bree. "Do we know who they are?"

She shook her head. "I doubt it. Darla? Do you know who owned this place?"

"We bought it from the bank. It had been foreclosed on. The previous owners left after a year and quit making payments on it. They were a young couple with a baby, so..." Darla hesitated. "I do know there have been at least five families to own this house, but I don't know anything about who they were or if there were more."

We headed downstairs, shutting the door on the two old ladies. I wondered if we could find the anchor that kept them there before they found a way to stop us.

CHAPTER NINE

GEORGIE ABSOLUTELY REFUSED TO GO DOWN IN THE
basement with us. "I can't. I can't do it—the place terrifies
me."

"That's all right," I told her, accepting a flashlight from
Darla. She handed one to Bree, too. "You can stay up here.
It's probably not a good idea for all of us to go down there, in
case something happens." I turned to Darla. "If you'd lead the
way?"

Darla reached for the knob and, before she could take
hold of it, the door swung open. She glanced at me and I
motioned for her to step behind me. Bree shook her head and
moved into the front. I let her take the lead—she was
stronger than I was and had faster reflexes.

Bree glanced around. "Do you have a doorstop? It occurs
to me that something might try to trap us while we're downstairs, and Georgie's not strong enough to go up against a
psychic force trying to hold the door shut."

Darla looked around. She picked up a hawk statue that
was cast in bronze. It had heft and weight to it. "What about
this?"

"It might work. We'll give it a try," Bree said, propping open the door. "Shall we?"

With Georgie waiting up top, we headed down the stairs, Bree going first, me coming after, and then Darla.

The basement was truly creep show–worthy. As we descended the narrow stairs, we had to hold onto the stone wall to the left. There was no railing, and the stairs were steep enough that one misstep would send us tumbling down headfirst. A bare bulb swung from the center of the basement below, its dim light serving to heighten the shadows behind the mass of boxes and clutter that crowded the room.

By the time we reached the bottom of the steps, I could see the compacted dirt that made up the top half of two walls. There was a hole in the dirt on one side, about a foot in diameter, and I wondered where it led to, and what—if anything—came through it.

Below the steps were shelves, with hundreds of empty mason jars lined up in rows. A few still had what must have been food in them, but the contents were bubbling, festering with bacteria. I didn't want to be around when enough gas built up for them to blow.

In the center of the room were the stacks of moldy cardboard boxes, along with several wooden trunks. I didn't want to touch anything down here—everything looked suspect and was covered with dust and spiderwebs. There was a fetid smell to the air, and the basement felt like it was closing in around us, exacerbating my fear of being trapped.

The last time I'd been in a room with this same feel was the day the Butcher captured Rian and me, and it took everything I had not to run back up the stairs. I was fighting both the fear of the present, and the all-too-vivid memory of the past.

"I suppose the best place to start is in the trunks," I said. "They look old and like they may have been here a long time."

As I spoke, a ripple raced through the room, like wind. Only there was no way for the breeze to get down here. In fact, I doubted that fresh air ever touched this space.

"This reminds me of some show on the Discovery channel—like when they find secret passages beneath a pyramid and follow it into a tomb, you know?" Darla shivered. "The energy's thick and feels like a combination of soot and grease. Let's get on with it so we can get out of here."

"Good idea," Bree said. "Are any of these your belongings?"

Darla shook her head. "No. There's no way I'd bring anything down here to store until this mess is junked. We *were* planning to clear out the basement first and finish it, but Kevin lost interest in the job a few days after we moved here."

"Whatever those two old women are—and I'm not entirely sure they're ghosts—they don't want this space cleaned out. If their anchor is down here, that would disrupt them." I knelt beside the nearest trunk and brushed away the cobwebs.

"E.G.T." The initials were branded on the wood. "Does that ring a bell?"

Darla shook her head. "No, it doesn't."

I examined the lock. "It's a simple padlock, but it's rusted. I doubt if we can find the keys. Do you have a crowbar? We can probably pry it open."

Bree jumped up. "I have one in my car. I'll be right back," she said, heading for the stairs.

"Should we go up, too?" Darla asked.

I shook my head. "No. She should be back soon."

As we waited, I became aware of every sound, every movement. There was a faint skittering sound in the hole in the wall. I shone my flashlight into the recess and saw glittering eyes looking back at me. But it was a mouse, and mice didn't scare me. At least it wasn't some demon-rat or whatever might be lurking in the shadows.

There was a faint dripping sound. Darla and I cautiously followed it through the piles of junk to find a pipe near one wall, running from upstairs through the ceiling, that was dripping to the basement floor. I frowned, searching for a crack, then realized it was condensation that had built up. I wasn't sure how it worked, but it looked relatively fresh, and the drip was so slow that the drops were drying before the tiny puddle grew larger.

"Oh, good grief," Darla said, peeking in one of the cardboard boxes. "It looks like there are stacks of *Jugs-A-Lug* in here."

"What's that?" I asked, turning to follow the beam of her flashlight.

There, on the top of one of the old cardboard boxes, was a magazine with a monster set of boobs staring down the camera. The woman's head wasn't visible, as though it didn't matter who it was, but the breasts were front and center.

"Well, the title doesn't lie," I said, snorting. "You say the box is full of those mags?"

"Yeah, looks like several years. From the 1970s, so it's been...oh geeze...fifty years? The pages are covered with mildew. I don't want to touch the crap down here. Mold in the air? Not good for the lungs. If we ever clear this house of whatever's haunting it, I may hire a mold specialist to come in and sanitize this room."

"Good idea," I said. Mold was to blame for a number of respiratory and auto-immune conditions.

At that moment, Bree returned, carefully descending the stairs with the crowbar. She went over to the trunk and I held onto the wooden box as she slid the crowbar under the lock. As she bore down on it, the lever managed to pry the lock away from the wood. A moment later, with a final grunt, Bree added all her weight to the bar and the lock broke off.

She moved back and nodded to me. I swung the lid up, trying to keep as much distance as I could between the trunk and me. I didn't want to be in the line of fire should there be some sort of magical trap.

As the lid opened, I looked inside. There was a jar filled with some dried herb, a large chunk of obsidian, a hand mirror, and two pairs of knitting needles, along with what looked like a half-finished potholder. I shone the light on the jar and read the label. "That's hellebore. It's used for numerous spells but one in particular involves summoning astral creatures, ghosts, and demons. That, together with the obsidian and the mirror, most likely has created a one-way portal in this house. Whoever placed this here was intent on keeping those two old women bound here—" I paused as a creaking sound came from the wall at the back of the basement, this side of the shelves beneath the steps.

Bree flashed her light over to the wall and we could see the faint outline of a door. "What the hell? Did you know that door was there?"

"No," Darla said. "I had no clue. We barely looked in the basement when we bought the house, to be honest. All we did was make sure there was no sign of water damage. In fact, it was Kevin who came down here to check it out."

Bree and I moved closer to the wall. We moved a couple of boxes away from the bottom of the door, and promptly a dozen huge brown spiders raced out, each with a leg span the width of my palm. Darla screamed and jumped back as I recoiled, but Bree brought her boot down on several of them as the others scuttled into the shadows.

"Crap, I hate those!" Darla exclaimed.

"I'm not fond of them, but at least they aren't poisonous," I said.

The giant European house spiders had thumbed a ride over from Europe on a boat bound for British Columbia, and they had spread throughout both western Canada and western Washington. They were freaking ugly, the second-fastest spider in the world—that we knew of—and they ran directly at you in their myopic quest to find mates. At least they ate hobo spiders. And hobo spiders were trouble.

Once the boxes were away from the door, I looked at Bree. She flashed her light around the edges of the door until we found an indentation near where the lock should be. It was deep enough to fit our fingers in, and there was enough of an overhang on the indentation to catch hold and pull.

"Ready?" Bree asked.

I nodded.

She carefully pulled the door open, standing back. I stood to the other side and motioned for Darla to move to the side so that nobody was a direct target should there be something or someone waiting for us on the other side.

As the door creaked open, the hinges complaining, I caught sight of some sort of mist inside. What the hell? Curious, I leaned forward, trying to peek around the side without offering whatever might be in that mist a clear shot at my head.

Bree flashed her light inside and gasped. "Look," she said, breaking the silence.

I followed her gaze and froze. There, in a small cubby, settled into two rocking chairs, were the skeletons of two women, and they were wearing the same outfits as our ghosts up in the attic.

"WHAT THE..." I stared at the skeletons, unsure of what to think. "Were they...who the hell put them in here?"

"I don't know," Bree said. "But look at their wrists and feet."

I brought my flashlight to bear alongside hers. The wrists of the skeletons were tied to the arms of the chairs. What looked like thick leather thongs held them fast. Or they would have been held fast, had there been flesh on the bones. The skulls still had bits of hair attached—one of them silver, while the other looked like a faded dark hair. The eye sockets disturbed me—there was a faint light in them, and that said "ghost" to me. But the skin was gone, the bones bare other than the hair, and there was no telling how long they'd been here.

"I think we'd better call the cops," I said. "If this was a murder scene, we shouldn't interfere. But before we do, I'm going to break this spell." I glanced back at the trunk. Beneath the needles and yarn was a piece of paper. I gingerly pulled it out, unfolding it. There, I recognized a series of runic inscriptions in Majekana—the secret language of witches. I scanned the writing.

Bind to bind, here you stay, forever now, and every day,
Bone to bone, I command you stay, forever now, and
*   every day.*
Herb to heart, heart to bone, I bind you here, to sit like stone.
Wrath to joy, and joy of wrath, forever trapped shall be your
*   path.*

What the hell? Someone had bound these two women to this house, but for what reason? Had they killed the old biddies, as well?

"I don't know what went down in this house, but I can break this spell by burning the paper. That doesn't guarantee they'll leave, but they'll be free to leave, although it may take more to get them out than that. They may like screwing with people. And the cops may want this incantation to put all the pieces together." I stared at the paper, frowning.

"Is there any other way you can break the spell?" Bree started to say but stopped as the entire house shook. The floor rolled under our feet.

"Quake? Get the hell out of this basement!" I wasn't sure how strong the foundation was and I wasn't about to stick around and find out.

Darla turned, tackling the stairs as the swaying continued. Bree pushed me in front of her and—as I used the wall to brace myself—she followed me up the steps. As we tumbled through the door up above, Georgie gave us a confused look.

"What's going on? Is something chasing you?"

Darla looked confused. "Don't you feel the earthquake?"

"No," Georgie said. "When did we have one?"

"Just a moment ago—the basement was shaking." Bree paused, then added. "You didn't feel anything?"

Georgie shook her head. "Not up here. All I heard was you guys suddenly shouting and then your footsteps on the stairs."

I dropped into a seat by the table. "If something can shake the basement, it can take us out. Bree, call the sheriff. Maybe I can talk her into letting me destroy that paper."

"I doubt it. Daisy runs things by the book unless there's a damned good reason. But yeah, we do need to call her. Skeletons in the closet, if they're as old as they look, aren't usually the typical stuff found in a basement." She put in a call. We decided that, having stirred things up, it might be prudent to wait out on the front porch for Daisy and her crew to appear.

TEN MINUTES LATER, Daisy Parker and several of her officers showed up, along with the coroner. We spent twenty minutes explaining the entire evening, the haunting, and what we found in the basement. Luckily, she took us seriously. As her men headed down into the basement, at least one of them let out a loud yip—he was a wolf shifter.

"Damn it, something pinched me, hard," he said.

I turned back to Daisy. "Sheriff, that's why I need this paper. I need to burn it to break the spell."

She took it from me and tucked it into a paper bag. "Sorry, I have to take this in as evidence. Can't you exorcise the spirits?"

"Not when they have an anchor downstairs. And when you collect everything and leave, that won't necessarily break the spell. I should salt the bones, or salt the anchor and burn that incantation. There aren't easy substitutes for houses that are haunted this badly."

"I don't know what to tell you," she said. "It's procedure. There are no statues of limitations on murder cases and, while this can't be ruled a murder yet—the women could have already been dead of natural causes when their bodies were put in that closet—the fact is that homicide can't be ruled out yet, either. If somebody murdered them, then I have to do my job." She looked frustrated.

I sighed. "Of course, yes—you need to do your job." I turned to Darla and Georgie. "Things may get worse. I recommend your family find a different place to live for a while. You might want to stay with friends."

"Will the ghosts follow us?" Georgie asked.

"I don't think so. I think they're anchored in the house."

Darla shook her head. "Kevin won't go for that. I can take the kids and leave, but he's not going to, I'll bet you anything," she said, staring at the floor.

I wasn't sure what to say to her, but at that moment, Kevin appeared at the door.

"What the hell is going on?" he asked, a storm cloud brewing in his expression.

"Kevin, this is Elphyra. She came over to deal with the ghost problems—" Darla started to say.

"Ghosts? We don't have any..." He caught sight of the sheriff. "And what the fuck are the cops doing here? What are you doing in my house?"

"We found two skeletons in the basement," Darla said, but he cut her off.

"You're shitting me. I had a long day at work, I wanted a night out with the guys and then to come home and relax, and this is what I find? Cops in the house? Strangers filling your head with this ghost bullshit? Darla, what the hell happened to making me happy? Where's my sandwich?"

"I'm sorry—" Darla started to say, blanching.

"Ease up, dude," I said, stepping in front of her. "The facts are these: you have entities in this house that want to *hurt* your family. You have two skeletons in your basement that were tied to their chairs and left there. And here you are, complaining about Darla not making you a fucking sandwich? Get real, for fuck's sake!" I had no use for gaslighters and whiny-assed men-children.

He stared at me. Then, before I could move, he back-handed me so hard I went reeling back against Bree and fell on my ass. My cheek stung, and I rubbed my bruised jaw as I jumped up, ready to tackle him. As I lunged, Daisy stepped in between us as two of her deputies tackled Kevin to the ground. He thrashed, shouting obscenities.

Bree examined my face. Darla and Georgie hurried over to me.

"How are you—" Bree started to say, but I waved her off.

I straightened my shoulders, wincing as I gingerly touched my cheekbone. I brought my hand away, my fingers slick with a trickle of blood. I turned to Kevin, who was being held in handcuffs between the two deputies, and gave a strong mental push and he let out a loud shriek and hunched over.

"Get this straight. Nobody, but *nobody* hits me and gets away with it. You try again and I'll nail your ass to the wall, literally. Be grateful I targeted your balls and not your head."

"Hold on!" Daisy brought a whistle to her lips and blew. The resulting sound echoed through the night air. "Elphyra, I'm going to let that one go, given he hit you first, but that's enough." She turned to Darla. "We're going to run him in for assault. You want to meet us there to bail him out?"

Darla let out a sigh. "Can I talk to you privately?"

Sheriff Parker motioned for her to step aside as the deputies carted Kevin away. The coroner and his team were headed into the house, and Georgie silently followed.

"I'll show you where to go, but I'm not coming down with you," she said.

I turned to Bree.

"I don't think they should be left alone with Kevin if he gets out. He's still entangled by the energy and frankly, I'm afraid for Darla and Georgie." I didn't want to think about what he could do to them under the influence of those two spirits.

"I'll talk to them and try to convince them to stay elsewhere. I have a feeling that's not going to be too difficult, given everything that's happened, and then seeing him deck you. You press charges, you hear?" Bree caught my gaze.

I nodded. "Yeah, I will. Maybe that will keep him locked up until we can exorcise whatever's in there." I glanced up at the ceiling of the porch. "I kind of wish this place would burn to the ground and take the skeletons with it. Purge them with flame."

"That's one way to solve it, but not possible. The skeletons will be headed to the morgue soon and so will all the evidence we found." Bree glanced back at Darla. The woman was still talking to the sheriff. "She looks so lost."

"I would be too. She's had her foundation ripped out from under her. Evil spirits—and they are evil—are controlling her husband, and they've taken over her home. Now, he's headed to jail for assault, and where's she supposed to go? I don't have any answers."

Bree patted me on the shoulder. "Let's take some pictures of your face for the cops and court. That should be enough to hold him for a few days, and maybe we can figure out how to exorcise the ghosts from the house and from him."

I sighed, but let her lead me over to better light, where she took pictures of my face. By that time, the coroner and his team were thoroughly enmeshed in their investigation. I gave the sheriff an account of what had happened, then—hugging Bree—I drove down to the station to sign the report pressing charges against Kevin. I'd given a subdued goodbye to Darla and her daughter, but I couldn't help but wonder if we had made things worse by finding the skeletons. If I'd only found the trunk, I would have burned the spell, but unfortunately, we found the bones that went with it, and that had changed everything.

CHAPTER TEN

BY THE TIME I UNLOCKED MY DOOR AND HAPPILY KICKED off my shoes, it was nearing ten P.M. and dark. I pulled into my driveway and stared at my house, grateful that I wasn't dealing with the house from hell that Darla had stumbled into. As I carried my things to the house, I looked up at the sky. There were clouds streaking the surface, but I couldn't sense any rain nearby. Content that the weather gods were quiet for the moment, I closed the door behind me.

May was reading a magazine, curled in the oversized recliner. She looked up as I dropped my purse on the coffee table and fell onto the sofa, sighing.

"Rough time?"

"That's an understatement." I stared at the ceiling for a moment, then sat up and pulled off my boots before crossing my legs beneath me. "Tonight has to be one of the spookiest nights I've ever had—well, barring...you know." I winced, gingerly touching the top of my cheekbone, where Kevin had hit me.

"What happened to you? You look like somebody punched you." May unwound herself from the chair and hurried over, cupping my chin and tilting my face up to get a better look. "Who did this? A ghost?"

I shook my head. "No, this is thanks to Darla's husband, who came home at an inopportune time and decided that he didn't like what was going on." I grimaced as she touched the wound. "That stings."

"Do you have a first-aid kit? Or at least Neosporin and bandages?"

"Yeah, in the bathroom. In the vanity—top left drawer."

She excused herself and within minutes, was back with the kit I always kept ready. "Come into the kitchen where I can get a better look of it."

I followed her into the kitchen and obediently sat at the table. "How's Fancypants? Where is he?"

"Sleeping off his dinner, and he's fine. He's going to be a spitfire, I tell you."

I laughed. "Good. I need a spitfire in my life."

May washed the injury and began poking around. "Does this hurt?"

"No," I said, as she pressed across where my sinuses were. Then she came to the edge of the wound. "Youch—now that hurts."

"I don't think he broke anything. But your eye is beginning to bruise up, so you're going to have a shiner. It looks like he caught you with a ring, to cause a gash like this. But you won't need stitches." She smoothed some of the antibiotic cream on it, then covered it with a bandage. "Let me get you some ice. Do you have an ice pack?"

"No, but I have a bag of frozen peas," I said, motioning to the fridge. "In the freezer."

She found the bag. Then, first putting a light tea towel over my cheek, she pressed the peas against it. "Here, hold this on your face for ten minutes."

I held the bag of peas against my cheek as I told her what

had happened. "You've lived in Starlight Hollow all your life, right?"

"Yes, I have."

"Do you remember two women who fit that description? Who might have gone missing?" It was a long shot, but worth asking.

She put the kettle on. "Hm. Tea?"

I shook my head. "I'm not a tea drinker, to be honest. But some bouillon would be nice. I have bouillon paste in the fridge." I loved chicken broth and drank it on a regular basis when I needed comforting.

May raised her eyebrows, but retrieved the jar and made me a mug of bouillon while she made herself some tea. "Let me think about the women. First, though, I should call Bran and let him know I'm almost ready. He's coming to walk me back to the house. I told him I'm fine, but with Olivia's death, he's on edge over me being out by myself."

"That's not a bad thing. It's amazing what can happen in a short time," I said, thinking back to Rian's death. "I'm glad he's looking out for you. Oh, by the way, there was a second murder. This time it was a man."

May frowned. "A second? Then it's not a one-off. That's worrying." She shook her head. "I'll call Bran."

While May called her son, I headed into the bedroom to peek in on Fancypants. He was curled up in the dresser drawer, on the floor near my bed, fast asleep. I wanted to wake him up because he looked so damned cute, but decided to let the little guy sleep. Returning to the kitchen, I put the peas back in the freezer, setting them to one side so I wouldn't absent-mindedly eat them. They could re-freeze for ice-pack duty without a problem, though.

May was waiting for me. "Bran will be here in a few minutes. I told him to drive over, since there's been a second death. Take no chances, you know. As far as the two old women...I vaguely remember a pair of sisters who annoyed everybody. They might fit that description, but that was years ago—when I was younger. That's the best I can do."

"I'm sure the coroner will be able to identify them. They still had their teeth. Of course, if they died prior to the advent of DNA analysis, that might not do any good."

The sound of a vehicle in the front announced Bran's arrival. I walked with May back to the living room as the doorbell rang. Taking no chances, I peeked through the peephole to see Bran standing there, and opened the door.

"Hey, thanks for coming to get your mom," I said. "I don't know if you'd heard, but there was a second murder this morning—a man."

His smile slipped as he stopped, reaching out to almost touch my face. He pulled his hand back, but said, "You okay?"

I shrugged. "I met a possessed man's fist. He didn't like me nosing around his house."

Of course, that made Bran sit down to hear the whole story. After I finished, he let out a low whistle.

"I hope that they keep him behind bars till those spirits can be exorcised—his wife and kids are prime targets. Say, you want me to come over tomorrow and help you plant those herbs?"

"You don't have to. You must have your own crops to tend to—" I started to say, but he interrupted.

"Don't worry about it. I'll be over at ten, if that isn't too early," Bran said.

I glanced at May, who was grinning, but she said nothing. "Well, if you're sure...I have an appointment at noon, though. Faron Collinsworth asked me if he could pick my brain about something."

Bran's demeanor shifted. His eyes narrowed as he cleared his throat. "What does Faron want with you? I thought wolf shifters and witches don't get along."

"We don't, generally. In fact, I've had two run-ins with Faron in the past couple days. But apparently something happened that he wants magical advice on. I told him to come over around noon." I suddenly felt like I had to explain myself and that I didn't like. "Whatever the case, it shouldn't take long."

"No problem," Bran said, standing. "I'll be done by noon." He escorted his mother to the door.

May turned back to me and winked. "I'll call you tomorrow to see how things are going with Fancypants. If you need me before then, text."

"Be sure to lock your doors after we leave," Bran reminded me. "And don't go out in the woods alone. Not with two people torn to bits."

I saw both of them out, waving as they drove away. As I closed the door and locked it, a noise behind me startled me and I whirled around. But it was Fancypants, flying out of the bedroom. He made a beeline for me and landed on my shoulder, staring at my face intently.

"You're hurt. Somebody hurt you." He leaned in to stare at my cheek. "Are you all right?"

"Yeah, I will be. May cleaned up the bruise and treated it." I didn't want to worry him. "So, here we are. You hungry?" I knew that kittens ate a lot when they were young, but I wasn't sure about dragonettes.

"Not yet. But soon, I'll need food," Fancypants said. "This is new...but...there are some things that feel familiar, though they're not."

I stared at him, as best as I could, given how close he was to my head. It would have been one thing had he been already hatched, but to see a creature so young with such a grasp on communication—it boggled my mind. He was a baby, yet he was as developed in communication as most adult humans. I was having a hard time wrestling with that concept.

"So...when you were in the egg, were you thinking like you are now?"

"I don't remember when it came on, but yes, at some point, I was self-aware. We mature in the egg, you know. There was a time when I became aware of what I was and I knew that the world outside existed. I can't explain what my thoughts were like—but at one point, I sensed you nearby and I knew you were my person. I knew that I needed to be near you. I called for you for a while before you heard me. But then you found me and everything worked out." He reached out and pressed his beak against my forehead. "And that's all that matters."

Still in awe of how dragonettes developed, I let it go. Maybe some expert had studied them and I could find a book on the subject to understand on a deeper level. And if not, did it matter? Fancypants was here, now, and my life had shifted because of him.

"So, what do you like to do? Or do you think you'll want to do, now that you're out of the egg?" Hearing my question, I snorted. "This has to be one of the oddest conversations I've ever had."

Fancypants snorted, too, turning away just in time to keep from blasting me with two small jets of fire. But I could feel the heat—it was very real, and I suddenly realized how dangerous it could be if he did that in my face.

"Pardon me! I didn't mean to do that!"

"Hey, be careful, okay? I don't want to lose my sight or deal with third-degree burns." I stretched my neck to the side, frowning.

"I said I'll be careful. I have no intention of hurting you," he said.

"Also, be careful shooting off fire inside. I like my house and want to keep it." I groaned, imagining him catching the curtains on fire. "Is there a way you can put a stop to breathing fire unless you consciously will it, or something? I'm now having visions of you setting the curtains on fire and burning down my house!"

Fancypants flew off my shoulder and settled on the coffee table. "I'm capable of controlling my flame, but if it makes you feel better, perhaps there's a process in which we can prevent accidental bursts."

I grabbed out my phone. "Maybe May's still up. She had a dragonette. She must have dealt with this."

MAY, IS THERE A WAY FOR A DRAGONETTE TO STOP SNORTING FIRE? I'M AFRAID THAT FANCYPANTS WILL BURN DOWN THE HOUSE WITHOUT MEANING TO.

A moment later, she texted back. YES, THERE IS—I HAD THAT PROBLEM WITH MELDA. WE FIGURED OUT A WAY TO MAKE IT A CONSCIOUS ACT RATHER THAN INVOLUNTARY RESPONSE. MUGWORT AND JASMINE WILL LESSEN THE PRODUCTION OF FIRE.

MUGWORT AND JASMINE?

YES. MIX FOUR DROPS OF MUGWORT TINCTURE WITH TWO DROPS OF JASMINE TINCTURE AND FEED IT TO HIM TWICE A DAY, MORNING AND NIGHT. THEY'RE WATER-BASED HERBS, AND THE MIXTURE WILL QUENCH THE RANDOM OCCURRENCE AND HE'LL HAVE TO THINK ABOUT CREATING FIRE IN ORDER TO DO SO. IT WON'T PUT A STOP TO THE PRODUCTION, BUT WILL MAKE IT A CONSCIOUS ACT.

I thanked her. "Well, we have an answer, but I'll have to either make the tinctures or buy them, if I can. Until then— just be careful?"

"Of course I'll be careful." He rolled his eyes. "Your house is safe."

"What do you want to do? I need to go to bed soon, but... do you need food?" I paused, then added, "If you have any questions about me—"

"No, I saw what I needed to see during the bonding." He

stopped, crooking his neck to look at me. "I know everything I need to know, and I will tell you this: I chose well." He paused, then added, "Elphyra, you deserve to be alive. You weren't the one to blame."

As he spoke, I knew—on a gut level—that he knew about Rian and what had happened. I caught my breath, trying not to tear up. Biting my lip, I tried to force the tears back, but they were so close to the surface that I was struggling to keep them at bay.

"His death isn't your fault. The blame belongs to the vampire." Fancypants's voice was surprisingly soft.

"I... I..." I didn't want to visit my pain on Fancypants. But he took wing, landing by my side. Awkwardly, he reached out and patted my hand. I stared down at him, wondering how someone so young and small could comfort me, but his touch was soothing. As the tears slid down my cheeks, he flew up and landed on my shoulder.

"You know what it's called," he said.

I nodded. "Survivor's guilt. My therapist explained it to me. But knowing something logically is different from being able to accept it on an emotional level. We were both tipsy, we both decided to walk home. It's not like I said, 'Let's go that way'...but it still happened and he sacrificed himself for me."

"He loved you," Fancypants said.

"I loved him, but I'm alive and he isn't." I hung my head, staring at my hands.

"Have you spoken to his spirit?" The dragonette fluttered his wings, wafting a strand of my hair back from my face.

I took a breath. "No. Why?"

"It might set your mind at ease." Fancypants frowned, or at least a good imitation of a frown. "You should eat. Your energy is disrupted by whatever happened this evening, and by your emotions right now."

I inhaled a long, slow breath, then counted to eight as I exhaled. The breathing exercises I'd learned as a girl stood me in good stead; they helped me calm myself when I felt on the edge of falling back into that abyss.

"You're right. Tonight was stressful and I was worried about the women I was trying to help. And then, getting punched didn't help matters any," I said. "You're right, I need some food." I stood and, with Fancypants leading the way, headed into the kitchen. I pulled out a can of tomato soup, the bread, butter, and cheese, to make soup and a grilled cheese sandwich, while the dragonette prattled. A few minutes later, as I was cooking, he had me laughing. I wasn't sure how, but he'd managed to lift my spirits in the matter of a few minutes. I prepared another meal for him and we sat together at the kitchen table, eating. And as odd as it was, everything felt perfectly normal.

CHAPTER ELEVEN

NEXT MORNING, I WOKE UP TO FANCYPANTS SITTING AT the end of the bed, staring at me.

"What?" I asked, squinting at him. "Why are you staring at me?"

"Time for breakfast," he said. "I can open the refrigerator, but I can't cook."

Grumbling, I sat up, pulling my hair out of my face. I glanced at the clock. "It's six A.M."

"Yes, time to be up and onto your day." He suddenly hiccupped and I heard a rumble.

"What's that?"

"My stomach," he said. "I need food..." He let out a gratuitous moan and gave me such a pathetic look that I sighed and threw back the covers, swinging my feet to the floor.

"You know how to work it, don't you?" I said, yawning. "All right, let me get my robe on and I'll make your breakfast." I went to the bathroom, washed my face and hands, and pulled my hair back into a ponytail. Then, with Fancypants chattering nonstop about some game show he watched while I was asleep, I trudged into the kitchen.

"What do you want for breakfast?"

"I don't know. I've only had ground meat."

"How about trying some scrambled eggs and toast?" I reached for a pan and then popped bread into the toaster. I could make one big pan of eggs and have my own breakfast, as well.

"I'll try it," he said, perching on the top of the paper towel roll. He paused, then added, "You aren't going to always call me 'Fancypants,' are you? The name's set now—there's no going back—"

"You mean I can't change it? I was reconsidering," I asked.

"Like the bonding, once a dragonette's been given a name, it's permanent. But you can call me whatever nicknames you like." He sniffed. "That smells good. Tell me, were the creatures that would have been born out of those eggs humanely killed?"

"They didn't even *form*. These are unfertilized chicken eggs. People eat unfertilized eggs."

Fancypants watched my every movement as I scrambled the eggs. I took them off the heat, then buttered the toast and divided the eggs onto two plates, cutting his toast into small chunks so he could pick them up. I carried breakfast over to the table, then made myself a latte.

"Me too?" Fancypants asked, sniffing the latte.

I stared at him. "You want caffeine? I don't know if it's good for you."

"No time like the present to find out," he said, staring at me with his glittering eyes. He'd never pull off the puppy dog look, but he was hard to resist.

"Look, this just..." I stopped, deciding that, since I was going to cave one way or another, I might as well save us both some time. "I'll make you a latte but if you get sick, you have yourself to blame. You understand?"

"I understand," he said as I pulled one shot and poured

milk and some sugar into it. I set the wide-mouthed mug down in front of the dragonette and stood back to watch. He sniffed it, cautiously stuck his tongue in it, then drained it like a thirsty frat boy at a kegger.

Within ten minutes, I knew we weren't going to repeat the experiment.

"Will you get down from there?" I yelled, staring up at the ceiling where Fancypants was riding one of the ceiling fan blades. "You're going to get dizzy and then you're going to—"

Before I could finish the thought, Fancypants leaned over the side of the blade and threw up, right onto the coffee table next to me. I jumped back to avoid the splash factor and walked over to the controls on the wall, where I turned off the ceiling fan. As it slowed, Fancypants lurched and fell off the blade. He was unable to take wing and I managed to catch him, though the effort knocked me back.

"For fuck's sake, what did I say?"

"That it wasn't a good idea," Fancypants said, his tongue lolling out of his mouth.

"And was I right?" I set him down on the sofa. "If you're going to throw up again, please notify me in advance."

"You were right, but what a ride!" He groaned and fell over on his side.

I was beginning to get worried about him now, so I pulled out my phone and called May. "Hey, is caffeine poisonous to dragonettes?"

She snorted. "No, but it makes them drunk. How much did he drink?"

"One shot of espresso," I said.

"That's akin to a human who can't handle his liquor drinking a twelve-pack of beer. You better put him to bed and let him sleep it off, once the jitters die down."

"Is there a danger he'll aspirate? He's already thrown up

once," I said. I had no desire for my dragonette to go the way of Jimi Hendrix, John Bonham, and Bon Scott.

"Probably not, but you can lay him on his stomach and make sure his neck is straight and his face hanging over a pillow." She sighed. "Don't let him talk you into things—they're good at that. And if they have a playful personality, they're likely to push you to go along with all sorts of things that they're better off not trying."

I sighed. "Well, he's out cold right now. Hopefully I didn't kill him."

"What are your plans for the day? Are you helping out your friend Darla?"

"No, there's nothing more I can do till they clear the crime scene. I did text her to let me know when that happens." I paused, then said, "So, Faron's coming over at noon. I'm still not sure what he wants to talk to me about and the more I think about it, the less sense it makes. Wolf shifters steer clear of our kind."

May laughed. "I know, but Faron never does anything without a reason. His testosterone is oozing out of his pores. But he's smart. He's the Alpha of his Pack for good reason. The man has brains."

I snorted. "Well, I guess that's saying something. Anyway, I'm going to clean house this morning. It was getting messy to start with, and now I have dragonette urp to clean up. Say, did Bran say he was coming over today? With all the chaos last night, I can't remember."

"Yes, in fact he's finishing up his breakfast and is about to head over to plant your herb garden. Honestly, he was so upset about you being punched last night that letting him do this will give him a sense that he's at least done something to help out. Bran's chivalrous, as old-fashioned as the notion might be. He's not a rescuer, thank gods—I couldn't take it if he brought home every woman who thought she was Cinderella, waiting for a prince to make everything all better. But Bran does stand by an honor code when it comes to women."

That was reassuring to hear. I didn't allow jerks and maggots—my inclusive term for all the misogynists, incels, gamer gaters, and male chauvinists out there—into my life.

"I'll see him when he gets here," I said. "Tell him I'll make him lunch. I'm a good cook, when I want to be."

As I hung up, I heard a faint burp. I glanced over at Fancypants, who was snoring. Luckily, in his sleep, he puffed out steam rather than smoke.

BY THE TIME I had cleaned up the dragonette vomit and started rinsing the dishes and putting them in the dishwasher, Bran showed up at my door. He was looking good this morning—better than I had remembered him—and was wearing a form-fitting tank top over jeans. His eyes sparkled and he flashed me a crooked smile.

"How are you doing? How's the eye?"

I shrugged. "The pain's down, though it's going to get uglier before it gets better. I haven't heard from Darla this morning. I'll call her later to see how they are."

"Well, if you're okay, then I'll get started. The herbs are by the workshop, it looks like?"

I nodded. I had lined them up outside the workshop to acclimate to the air. "Yeah, they are. I'll come help in a bit as soon as I finish vacuuming." I detested housework, but it needed to be done. I disliked dust and clutter even more.

"No hurry," he said. He clattered down the stairs and headed over to the workshop. I watched him go. He was comfortable in his body, it was easy to tell by the way he moved.

I went back to my chores. Once a week, I cleaned the house, and—on a different day—once a week I did the laundry. It kept things from piling up.

As I washed the counters, I thought about the official opening for my business. I'd waited long enough for the licenses, and now I had them. I had the space, and I had all the supplies I needed. I just needed to get them in order and hang up my shingle.

So why don't you? You could have had everything ready by the time the business license arrived.

I didn't like it when my brain kicked out facts to me like that. I folded the kitchen towel and hung it over the range handle, then sat down at the table with my day planner, doodling as I forced myself to face the fact that I was afraid.

What if I can't make it? What if I'm not good enough? Both were frightening thoughts. But then that annoying voice whispered again, *You know that's not the reason. What's the real reason you haven't gotten off your ass yet?*

I thought it over for a bit. What was I afraid of? It couldn't be success—I was driven and ambitious. That was one of the things Rian had loved about me—my drive and my goals. He had been my biggest cheerleader and it tore me up that he wasn't here to watch me carry out my dream. Of course, I'd planned on doing this in Port Townsend—opening an herb and spell shop—but regardless of where it was, I was still on track.

And then it hit me. He wasn't here to see me do this... Rian wasn't here and I was moving into my future without him. I was moving on, and that meant *I was leaving him behind.*

"Oh gods," I said, pressing my hand to my lips as my stomach knotted. By moving ahead with my life, I was leaving him in the past and that meant his death was real—he wasn't going to magically come back into my life. He wasn't going to reappear to create a fairytale ending to a nightmare of a story. *"Rian..."*

"Are you okay?" Fancypants flew into the room, a worried look in his eyes. He settled down on the table, beside me.

"Yeah, I'll be fine," I said, wiping my eyes. "This is why waterproof mascara and eyeliner come in so handy," I tried to quip, but my voice cracked and I stared at the table.

"You're not okay," Fancypants said.

"I will be, I promise. I was just remembering..." I paused. I didn't want to go into it again—every time I talked about Rian's death, it stabbed another dagger in my heart.

After a moment, Fancypants said, "All right. Can you open the door for me? I'd like to go outside."

"You'll be careful? There are hawks and eagles out there and they'd probably love to make their lunch off a baby dragonette like you." I gazed at him, trying to assess whether he was strong enough to fight them off.

"I can hold my own. Don't worry about me. I'll be fine. Singed feathers make for wary opponents." He snorted and this time, two jets of fire appeared. They weren't huge but I had the feeling he was reining himself in.

"All right. Don't go far, okay?" I opened the kitchen door and he flew out and headed over toward Bran. I watched him for a moment, then returned to the table. I sat down and opened the planner. I hadn't used it since I moved here, but now I swallowed my tears and decided it was time to set a firm date for opening my shop.

I glanced at the calendar. It was mid-June, and I could have the shop pulled together within a couple weeks, tops. But I had to also make up spell kits and charms, and those took time and magical energy. July fourth was coming up and that meant people would be heading out for campouts and parties, so I decided to give myself a month and open the shop on July thirteenth—a Saturday. I planned to be open Tuesday through Saturdays, from ten A.M. through four P.M., and I'd take Monday off. Since I still had plenty in savings from my inheritance, I didn't want to overload myself.

I circled the thirteenth with a big red line and stared at the page, letting it sink in. Putting it in the calendar made it real. This was it—I was doing this. I pulled out a new notebook and opened it to a blank page. Then, using asterisks to mark off each task, I began to list everything I'd need to do to be ready.

TWO HOURS LATER, Fancypants was back, lounging on the sofa, looking bored, and I was making lunch for Bran. I wanted to get it out of the way before Faron arrived. The way he had acted the night before had warned me that they might not get along together. As I carried the sack containing a turkey sub, an apple, and four cookies out to him, I was pleasantly surprised to see that he had managed to plant almost all of the herbs, and to label them with white stakes. The beds were lovely and it would be a breeze to keep up with them.

"Thank you!" I said, setting the lunch bag on the corner of one of the beds. They were filled with every herb I could think of to buy, and I noticed he had arranged them in four sections: culinary herbs, culinary herbs that could be used for magic, strictly magical and medicinal herbs. And even a section for baneful herbs. "This is wonderful. You've done a fantastic job."

He stood back, beaming, folding his arms over his chest. "I'm glad you like it. I tried to pattern them in what seemed like the most logical order to me." He glanced at his phone.

"It's almost eleven. Is there anything else you need me to get to before I have to leave?"

I handed him his lunch. "Not that I can think of. Stick around if you like. I finally decided on an opening day for my shop next month. I need to have a sign made to hang at the end of my driveway, and another one to go over the shed. I should also create a graveled parking space for cars, don't you think?"

He scanned the area around the workshop. To the left was the utility shed, which sat near the treeline. To the right was the lawn extending to the beginning of the circular driveway.

"I think over there would be best, so they can park right off the drive and not interfere with your parking spaces for friends and family. Also, it creates a bit of a distance between them and your house—an unspoken boundary." He paused, then asked, "Do you have a restroom in the workshop so your customers don't have to enter your home?"

I nodded. "A powder room, yes. I asked the contractor who renovated the workshop for me to install one. I also have a sink in the main workshop for washing herbs and other things. I had him build walls so the workshop part is private and away from the area that will serve as the store. All I have to do at this point is stock the shelves and put up the signs."

"I can make your signs, if you don't have someone in mind yet." Bran stared at the workshop. "What do you want them to look like?"

"You don't have to—" I stopped at his look. He wanted to help. It occurred to me that Bran was a man so caring that it would be easy to take advantage of him. While he wasn't a pushover, his big heart might get him in trouble. He was lucky he'd been strong enough to avoid having his heart broken so far—though his ex-girlfriend had done a good job of jerking him around.

"I don't have to what?" he asked.

"If you're going to go to all the trouble to make my signs, I insist on paying you for the work. You are a generous man and I won't take advantage of you. I was going to have to pay for them anyway and this way, at least I know who's doing the work, instead of hiring somebody on Designarama."

Designarama was a website for artists of all types to sell their wares. The vendors ranged from those who made cringy home-crochet cock cozies to artists who could put the great masters to shame. The main criterion was that all products sold had to be original art, whether it be digital wallpaper or tea cozies. No mass-produced items were allowed, nor AI-generated art.

"I'm pretty handy with signage," he said. "Meanwhile, I have another hour or so. I noticed that you have a bunch of shelving to install in the utility shed?"

"The shelves go in the workshop, in the sales area. I have everything marked out on the walls. If you want to help me by installing them, I'd appreciate it. But I can't let you work for free," I said. "The only friend I'm willing to take advantage of is Bree. She and I have an understanding. We're there for each other, if at all possible. Please, how much would you charge?"

He sighed. "How about this: I'll install your shelves and gravel your parking area for five hundred, which will include the gravel and anything else I need to buy."

I knew that I wouldn't find a better price. "That's more than fair."

"I'll work till noon, then get home to take care of the farm. It will probably take me several mornings to finish, if that's all right. Then I can get to the signs." He pulled out a handkerchief and wiped off his brow. Sweat beaded on his upper lip and it took everything I had to keep from reaching out to wipe it away.

"That sounds good," I said. "I'd better—" I paused as the sound of a car approached.

Bran and I both turned as the Ford truck pulled into the driveway. The door opened and out jumped Faron Collinsworth, and as he and Bran stared at each other suspiciously, my mouth ran dry.

CHAPTER TWELVE

"Faron," I said, walking over to greet him.
"Welcome to my home. Do you know—"

"Oh, we know each other," Bran said. He straightened,
staring impassively at Faron.

Faron met his gaze with a bemused smile and extended
his hand. "Bran, so good to see you again." While the tone of
his voice was pleasant, he too had straightened and stood
unnaturally stiff. He was wearing a polo shirt fit to his trim
waistline, blue jeans, and motorcycle boots. His hair was
hanging loose, sleekly brushed. Not a strand was out of place.

I wondered what had gone down between the two, but
wasn't about to ask.

After a moment, Bran took Faron's hand and gave it a
brief shake, then glanced over his shoulder at the garden. "I'd
best get back to my work. I'll put up those shelves now."
Before I could say a word, he turned and walked away.

I watched him go for a moment, then turned to Faron,
feeling oddly embarrassed. I wasn't the one who had been
incredibly rude but I still felt awkward, given it was my land
and house.

"So..." I wasn't sure what to say. I had been brought up to welcome guests into the house with a dinner plate and a glass, and neither ever stayed empty. That had changed since the Butcher, but the graciousness my mother had shown friends and family when I was young had stuck. "Come in, please. Welcome to Thornwylde, my home and land."

Faron hesitated, then graciously nodded and followed me toward the house. It was then that I remembered Fancypants. "Hold on, please. One moment!"

He stopped as I raced into the house. Fancypants was sitting on the sofa, watching TV. He gave me a quizzical look as I raced in and slammed the door behind me.

"You need to hide. Someone is visiting and I don't want him knowing about you. I don't know him well enough to trust him yet." I glanced around, trying to figure out where to stash the dragonette.

"I'll stay in the bedroom." Fancypants flew up into the air and hovered in front of me. "You aren't taking him in there, are you?"

I snorted. "Not likely. Go."

Without a word, Fancypants turned and flew sedately into the bedroom. I followed, closing the door. Then, I hurried back to the front door and opened it. "Sorry, come on in. I had to pick up a few things."

I didn't want Faron to know about Fancypants. I had no clue how trustworthy the wolf shifter was, and I wasn't about to find out with something as important as Fancypants's existence. The fact that I had a dragonette wasn't up for public knowledge. I would tell Bree, of course, and May and Bran already knew, but other than that, I'd have to carefully choose who I told about his existence.

Faron looked around. "Where should I sit? Do you want me to take my shoes off?"

I glanced at his feet. His boots looked relatively clean.

"Not necessary. Please, have a seat on the sofa. Would you like something to drink? I have some lemonade and cola in the fridge."

He shook his head. "That's all right. I'm fine. Thank you anyway." He stiffly took a seat on the sofa and waited. I sat down in the rocking chair that was kitty-corner the sofa and let out a long breath.

If we kept on like this, he'd be here until January.

"So, what did you want to ask me?"

"Right to the point, I see," he said, smiling for the first time.

"Well, we don't exactly have a great history, so I'm surprised you wanted to come over." I snorted. "By the way, I'm sorry about running into your shopping cart."

"It was an accident. No harm done." He sat for another moment, then let out a loud sigh and said, "You're right. So here's the reason I wanted to talk to you. I have a problem and I need a witch's opinion with regards to it."

"What about May and Bran? Why aren't you asking them?"

Faron shrugged. "You saw how Bran reacted? I don't tend to approach him or his mother. They aren't my biggest fans."

"Okay...and you don't know any other witches?"

He paused, then said, "You know how witches and wolf shifters react to each other. You're new here and, except for the two times we've run into each other, you haven't formed an opinion of me. At least, I am hoping you haven't."

I thought about it for a moment. I could be an asshole about this and tell him to leave. But something about him told me that—below that gruff exterior—lurked a genuinely decent man. The animosity between wolf shifters and witches stemmed from their innate fear of our magic, but I decided that—given he had come to me—he might be able to set that aside.

"All right. Ask away and I'll answer if I can—or if I choose to."

Looking relieved, he said, "Have you heard about the two murders that happened recently?"

I blinked. I hadn't expected the conversation to turn in *this* direction. "You mean Olivia? I don't remember the other person's name, but I think it was a man."

"Right, those murders. The coroner thinks a shifter is at fault, and he specified that he suspects a wolf shifter from my Pack. I know *every* member of the pack. As the Alpha—their King—nothing gets by me. And I know that no one in my Pack is guilty. But the sheriff has set her sights on one of my lieutenants. Elroy may be hotheaded, and he goes off half-cocked sometimes, but he's not a killer." Faron shook his head. "He's a handful, but I've known him since he was a pup. He might get in a few brawls, but he'd never hurt a woman, let alone kill her. The same goes for the man."

I sat back, wondering what I could do. "All right, but why did you come to me? How can my magic help you?"

"Witches can talk to ghosts, and they can also see through deception, right?" Faron sounded so sincere that I realized he truly believed both things.

"Some of us can talk to ghosts, yes, but not all. As for seeing through deception...if I had that power, I'd be rich. But...let me get this straight. What you're asking me to do is to see if I can find Olivia's ghost and ask her who killed her? I'm sure if the cops had that capability, they'd have the killer in hand, right?" I didn't want to burst his bubble, but it only made sense that the cops would have already thought to bring in somebody who could hunt down the ghosts and talk to them about it. And if they *had*, maybe that's why they had their sights set on Elroy.

"I suppose," he said. "But would they actually do that? Testimony from spirits isn't admissible in court. Why bother if you can't prove to the judge who did it?" He leaned forward, resting his elbows on his knees.

"Honestly? To give them an idea of which direction to look. If they think they know who their suspect is, then they could search for the actual evidence to support the suspicion. Did you ask Sheriff Parker if she's talked to someone about that?" I wasn't sure that I wanted to insert myself in a murder case, regardless of how small of a part I'd play.

He shook his head. "No. The sheriff doesn't like me. Her eye's always glued on my community. The local Puma Pride doesn't care for the Olympic Wolf Pack."

From hanging out with Bree so long, I knew that the puma shifters tended to view the wolf shifters as a bunch of thugs. The feline shifters saw themselves as more intelligent than most of the other shifters. It was a genetically based bias more than anything, and though science had proven the opinion wrong, on a cultural basis the belief was widely prevalent.

"Well, I can't argue with you there. I do know the bias exists," I said.

"Right. So how can I be sure they're examining all angles? I know Parker's a decent person, but what if she's letting her instinctive dislike for my kind affect her? She might not even realize what she's doing."

Faron made another good point. "All right, I'll call the sheriff and ask if they've had someone in to search for the victims' ghosts." I stared at him. He really was a good-looking guy, and he seemed to be an alpha without being an asshole, like I had first thought.

Leaning back against the sofa cushion, he said, "Thank you. I appreciate any help you can give us." He glanced around the room. "This is nice. I've never been here, but I pass by on my way to my sister's house."

"Doesn't she live out in your compound? I thought all wolf shifters lived in one neighborhood."

"Not all. Those belonging to other packs don't live out in the Shifter Village. Those from my Pack do, for the most part, but there are exceptions. My sister married outside of the Pack, and her husband didn't want to live by the rules of the Village."

"He's not a shifter?"

"No, he's not. He's human. They live about five miles up the road from here, near Quilcene. They have three children —fraternal triplets. Matt and Sue have been married for ten years. I go out to visit and play with my nephews every couple weeks. They're nine years old."

I wasn't sure how the genetics worked. "Are the children shifters? Can you be half-shifter? You can be half-Witch and inherit some or all of the magical genes."

"No, actually. Or rather, it's very rare for someone to be half-shifter. Two of the boys inherited the shifter genes, and I'm helping them learn how to hunt. The third boy—Ben—is human like his father. But he got the brains. He's a genius and the school has skipped him ahead so that he's going to start high school this fall." Faron stopped, as though suddenly aware he'd been talking up a storm. The pride and love he had for his nephews was evident with every word he said.

I smiled, ducking my head so he wouldn't think I was laughing at him. "That's pretty impressive. What's your sister like?"

Faron shrugged. "Sue always has been the rogue of the family. She's still a member of the Pack, but only because I'm her brother. When she fell in love with Matt, our parents were pretty pissed about it. But since they live in a different state, and I've been the Alpha for a while, they left it to me to deal with it. They're slowly coming around, though, the longer that Sue and Matt are together and they see that he treats her like a queen."

It made me sad to hear that his parents had turned their back on their daughter. But in some shifter communities, it was tradition, and tradition was hard to buck. At least it sounded like they were open to change.

"I'm glad you're still friends with her," I said, not knowing why I cared.

Faron studied me for a moment. "Yeah, me too."

"Listen," I said. "About the sheriff. Doesn't Elroy have an alibi? Why is the sheriff looking at him as a suspect?"

That elicited a response. Faron burst out cursing. "Fucking idiot likes to run off alone in his wolf form without telling anybody. He was out gallivanting around, and he didn't tell anybody where he was going, or that he was even *going to go* out for a run. His girlfriend isn't any smarter, and she wasn't with him to provide an alibi. My Pack is trained to tell the truth, Elphyra. They know better than to lie to me."

He leaned forward, clasping his hands. "Truth is, I'm afraid that Daisy could railroad Elroy. She doesn't care for us, and he has no alibi. But he doesn't have any motive either. I've asked them to perform DNA tests, to see if there's any of his DNA at the scenes. I'm *that* confident he's innocent."

"If he's so chaotic, why is he one of your lieutenants? I'm not sure how rank works in the wolf shifter packs, but I wouldn't think to put someone who's that erratic in a position of power." I glanced at the grandfather clock. It was going on quarter of one. It wasn't like I had any pressing appointments, but this had been an awkward meeting.

Faron cleared his throat. "He's good at his work and he's loyal." He paused again, then added, "Okay, I'm going to ask even though it's none of my business. Where did you get the shiner? Who the hell hit you? If you need me to, I'll go after him. Was it Bran?"

Startled by the suggestion, I stiffened. "Bran? No! He wouldn't... No, my black eye's the result of being a good Samaritan. I'm working on a haunting, and the husband's possessed. He decked me. Except it wasn't him—it's the entity who's possessing him."

"Bran's not as polite as you might think," Faron said. "He's been involved in more than one altercation with a couple of the men in my Pack. But as for the man who hit you—you said he's possessed?"

I nodded. "Full on *Exorcist* Linda Blair style. I'm worried about his family, to be honest. I'd better call them soon and see how last night went." I waited, but he showed no signs of getting ready to leave. "Well...is there anything else?"

Faron stared at me for a moment, then it seemed to register. "Oh! No. Please contact me when you've talked to the sheriff. Even if she isn't interested in hunting down the ghosts, I could hire you to do so. Maybe if *we* know who committed the murders, then we can find a way to convince her that Elroy is innocent." He sounded so hopeful that I caved.

"All right, hold on. Before you go, I'll call the sheriff and see what she has to say." I retrieved my phone and called Daisy. I wasn't fond of dealing with the authorities, but Faron seemed so positive, and I didn't want to see anybody railroaded for a crime they didn't commit.

Daisy answered after the third ring. "Sheriff Parker here."

She was abrupt and to the point, but I figured niceties were a luxury, especially since she was dealing with a couple murders.

"Hi, this is Elphyra," I said, not sure how to begin.

"Oh, hey. If you're calling about Kevin—"

"I'm not, actually. Though I'd be interested in what's going on. I haven't heard from Darla today." Once we disturbed those skeletons, there had to be some sort of repercussion.

"We had to turn him over to the psychiatric ward at the Peninsula Hospital. During the night, he had what looks like a psychotic break. The guards had to call in the medics and they decided to take him to the hospital psych ward. They're holding him until they can figure out what's going on, and he'll be remanded to us once he's...back to himself."

I wasn't sure what to say. I knew *exactly* what was wrong with Kevin—he was possessed. But while some medical centers recognized that as a legitimate condition, not all did. Especially those who were human-focused rather than Otherkin-focused.

"Well, I can tell them what's wrong, though I don't know if they'd believe me." I paused, then added, "But that's not why I called. I'm calling with a question about the murder cases you're working on. With Olivia and...what's the other guy's name?"

"Lucius Jackaberry. He was a witch. What do you want to know?"

I sighed, glancing over at Faron. "Have you by any chance asked a witch to see whether they can find the ghosts of Olivia and Lucius? If you can talk to them—if they're still around—maybe that would give you a leg up on the killer." I wanted to tread carefully, so that she didn't kick me out of the loop for being too nosy. At least not until I knew what was going on.

"We have a suspect, but in answer to your question: no, we haven't. I don't know that it's necessary. The suspect has no alibi for either murder, he fits the profile, and we've uncovered evidence pointing to him having a beef with one of the murder victims." She hesitated, then said, "Collinsworth asked you to look into this, hasn't he?"

"Yeah," I said. I wasn't going to lie. "He did. He seems so positive—"

On one side, Faron suddenly was trying to shush me, he was frantically waving his finger in front of his lips, and on the other side, Daisy laughed. It was a rough laugh, but a laugh nonetheless.

"I thought so. He's been calling me every hour, trying anything he can think of to shake me off his friend's tail." The irritation shone through Daisy's voice.

I cleared my throat. "But doesn't he have a point? If the ghosts are still hanging around and they corroborate your theory, then that's just extra evidence. And if they have a different story...well, the last thing you want is to jail an innocent man, isn't it?"

She was silent for a moment, then sighed. "All right. If you're volunteering. I can't pay you. However, you need to take one of my men along with you to verify that you actually went to those areas. You know that we can't use a spirit's testimony in court—obviously there's no good way to validate what you say you heard, and it would be hearsay anyway. But we *can* use it in our investigation. Are you free at four o'clock today?"

"Yeah," I said, suddenly realizing that I had landed myself in the thick of it.

"I'll have Arnie Fryer pick you up and take you to the murder scenes. I also don't want you going alone while the killer is still out there." She added, "If that's all, I'm swamped. I'll talk to you later." And just like that, she disconnected.

I stared at the phone for a moment, then turned to Faron. "Well, it looks like I'm going to check out the murder scenes later today. I'll let you know what I find out, if anything."

He stared at me for a moment, and I wasn't sure what he was thinking.

Then, he said, "Would you go out to dinner with me

tonight? We can talk over what you found and...I owe you one since I was so rude to you, and now here you are, helping me."

His dark eyes flashed with a dangerous flare, and I caught my breath, my stomach fluttering. We had somehow just fallen into dangerous territory.

"Thank you, but I'm not sure that's a good idea," I said.

"Oh, come on," he said, grinning. "What can it hurt?"

I could think of a lot of reasons *not* to go out with Faron Collinsworth, but inside, that voice I listened to all too often whispered, *Go*. And so, with a feeling that I was getting myself in deeper than I wanted to, I agreed to go out to dinner with him.

"I'll pick you up at eight," he said, as he strode toward the door. "I'll see you tonight."

I closed the door behind him, and my thoughts derailed on me.

Beneath the worry, I found myself wondering what his chest looked like under that shirt. Did he have a six-pack? Was his skin smooth or did he have chest hair?

Trying to shake off the feelings that were stirring deep inside, I forced myself into the kitchen and fixed lunch for Fancypants and me. But in the back of my mind, I knew that I was playing with fire. And I knew that for the first time in months, I wanted to touch the flame.

CHAPTER THIRTEEN

"WHAT THE HELL DO I DO?" I HAD BREE ON THE PHONE AS I nibbled on the roast beef sandwich I'd made. Bran had gone home without saying goodbye, so I was saved him asking what Faron and I had talked about. I could imagine what he would say if he knew about my date with the wolf shifter. Fancypants had almost eaten his weight in cat food and had gone to sleep it off.

Bree sighed. "Hold on." She muted the phone. A couple minutes later, she returned. "Okay, I can talk for a few minutes. Where's he taking you?"

"I forgot to ask. He said he'd meet me here. He said he felt he owed me one, but is that the only reason he's taking me out?" I couldn't bring myself to say *Do you think he's interested?* It felt so wrong.

"Faron Collinsworth doesn't waste time on things and people who don't interest him. This is a date. I guarantee you, it's not a thank-you for going out to see the ghosts. Which sounds terrifying, by the way, and thank you for not volunteering me to go with you. Last night was more ghostbusting

142

than I ever signed up for." She snorted. "No, Faron asked you out for a date. Nothing less."

I carried my phone and what was left of my sandwich into the bedroom and settled down at my vanity. I wanted to be comfortable for poking around in the woods. I set the phone across a tall pillar candle to hold it up so the speaker would catch my voice, and stared at myself in the mirror.

"Okay, now second question. What should I wear to go hunt down these two ghosts—" I stopped as my phone announced another call. It was the sheriff. "I'll call you back. Daisy's calling me right now."

I switched over to the other call. "Hey, Sheriff Parker. What's up?"

I divided my hair into three sections and began to braid it so it wouldn't catch in any bramble bushes if we had to wade into the undergrowth.

"Call me Daisy. I have a feeling we're going to end up on a first-name basis eventually." She paused, then added, "There's been another murder. We received the call five minutes ago. I'm headed out the door as we speak. Arnie will be at your place in forty-five minutes. He'll bring you to the new scene first. I thought you might have better luck with a fresh victim —" She stopped abruptly, then sighed. "I didn't mean to be so blunt. But isn't it true that you stand a better chance of talking to a spirit shortly after they've been murdered or died?"

"I don't know the answer to that," I said, my heart plummeting. The last thing I wanted was to see a mutilated body. I knew what one looked like, and the memory was all too fresh. But now, I felt a certain sense of responsibility. Three people had been butchered, and I had the opportunity to not only help the cops find the killer, but to potentially prove a man was innocent. I didn't want Elroy to end up in prison if he had nothing to do with their deaths.

"I'll be waiting," I said. As Daisy hung up, I called Bree again, thinking that pretty soon I was going to owe her for playing therapist.

TEN MINUTES LATER, Fancypants was awake and hovering over the table as I drank another latte. "You'll be careful, won't you? Can I have one of those?"

I glanced up at him. "Will you please land? You're making me nervous, fluttering so close to my head. And no more caffeine for you. We've been down that route and it wasn't pretty. You'd be divebombing me before you were done."

"Well, excuse me for flying," he said, but he landed on the top of the centerpiece—a candelabrum—balancing on it with perfect precision. "So, there's a murderer out there and you're going to try to help catch him. That makes me nervous."

"Not exactly," I said. "I'm trying to help *the cops* catch a murderer. And I'll be careful. I know what it's like to worry about somebody."

I hadn't told Fancypants about Rian, but I suspected the bonding process went deeper than he had let on. I was finding that I seemed to know more about dragonettes than I should. And he knew things about me that he shouldn't have.

"Hey, can you read minds?" I asked.

He coiled his head, staring at me with those crystal blue eyes. "No. But I do sense things about you that you might try to keep private." He added, "I know that you lost your mate and that made you incredibly sad."

I sighed. "I thought you might. I'm sorry. I've got a lot of baggage."

"Don't apologize," Fancypants said. "It's all part of the process." He hesitated. "I think it's good you're going to dinner with the wolf man tonight. It will do you good, more than you can imagine."

"I don't know about that," I said, "but I promise to be careful out in the woods today. I don't intend to take any more chances than necessary." As I finished my drink, I suddenly thought of something. "Hey, I don't know if this is a sore spot—if it is, forgive me—but do you remember your mother? Do you know who she is? Do you ever meet your families?" Even as I asked, I realized that I knew that Fancypants had never met his mother and had no idea where she was.

"Vaguely—there's this sense that she's still alive. I would know her if we were to meet—even without being introduced. But as to her name, or knowing the specifics of where she is? No. I don't know. We live our lives in relative obscurity. Dragons—our larger cousins—have the need to be known and revered. Dragonettes don't. We understand our worth, but we also prefer staying in the shadows. We're creatures of the forest, where dragons are creatures of the mountains and air."

I thought about that for a moment. "Are there dragons connected to the water—and to flame?"

Fancypants gave me a bob of the head. "You begin to understand. We're all connected to the elements. There are water dragonettes. They can't fly, but they swim deep and swift. They're reminiscent of eels, with a larger body and fins. And there are fire dragonettes, who mostly live around volcanoes. You can also find them appearing near wildfires. They seldom come over from Sescernaht, because they cannot live without heat. Most of the dragonettes who live in your realm are forest, water, or air based."

"Does your color depend on the element you're connected with?" It seemed odd to me that a forest dragonette would be red.

"No," he said. "Dragonettes come in all colors, and you can't discern our element by the color of our skin. Our coloring is random. While a dragonette can lay a clutch of eggs and they might all be different colors, the babies will connect to either the element of the mother or father. There are no half-breeds."

"So, either your mother or father or both had to be an earth dragonette?"

"Correct," Fancypants said. "As to which parent we take after, it's random. And within a clutch, each egg will be either one or the other—they don't have to all be the same unless both mother and father were from the same element."

I finished my latte. "Will you be all right while I'm gone tonight?"

"Of course. Just leave me food for a snack, if you would." Fancypants twined his neck, waving it like a snake. It was both mesmerizing and beautiful, like a dance.

"All right, but if something happens—"

"It won't. Go and enjoy yourself. Or rather, enjoy yourself tonight. I rather doubt you'll enjoy hunting for a ghost next to a fresh body."

I snorted. "Right, thanks for reminding me. I'm *so* looking forward to this."

Arnie was due to arrive in fifteen minutes. I looked for something to do. The house was clean—I liked order and I never let clutter build up, so I told Fancypants that I'd be outside, and set out a snack of dry kibble along with water for him.

I was nervous, and one of the reasons was that a little part of me was afraid that the killer might be spying, hidden away. And if so, would they target me, thinking the ghosts told me who they were? I tried to walk off my nerves by looking in on my new herb garden.

The raised beds were beautiful, the smell of the plants

filtering through my senses. I could smell the basil and the sage, the dusty scent of thyme. The sprouts of dill were tiny, but they were growing. Everywhere around me, I could feel the emergence of new life, the burgeoning awareness of the movements of the sun and moon, the approach of the rain, as the young plants dug their roots deep and spread their leaves.

I ran my hands over the leaves, my magic intermingling with the magic that came from all living beings bound to the earth by root and tendril. Crystals and stones had a different sort of bond with the Mother, and I cherished that connection as well. But there was something about plants—they had that spark of life to them. Stones were sentient in a different way. Almost alien, they sensed life through the slow drip of time, the creeping hands that passed on a geological level. Plants needed water and air for life, and the sun. Stones could live in a vacuum.

A moment later, the sound of tires on gravel alerted me and I turned around. A deputy stepped out of a sheriff's car. He hesitated when he saw me, then started over my way. I saved him the trip and hustled to his side.

"Deputy Fryer?" I asked.

"One and the same," he said, inclining his head as he tipped his hat. He was a pleasant-looking fellow, with short black hair and hazel eyes. "Ms. MacPherson?"

I nodded. "Call me Elphyra. Let me grab my purse."

I hurried back into the house, where I found Fancypants curled up in the corner of the sofa. "Would you like me to turn on the TV?" I asked.

He crooked his neck and let out two puffs of smoke. "Do you have a nature channel?"

I nodded. "GeoEarth—the shows are situated around science, animal, and nature documentaries. Will that work?"

Fancypants shifted, looking interested. "Yes, thank you. I believe it will."

I took hold of the remote, turned on the TV, and found the channel. "I'll call May and ask if she can come up at some point to make sure everything's okay." Although Fancypants seemed perfectly capable of taking care of himself, I still didn't want to worry. As I waved goodbye and left the house, locking the door after me, I texted her.

MAY, CAN YOU COME OVER AND CHECK ON FANCYPANTS? I'LL BE GONE ALL AFTERNOON AND EVENING AND I'D RATHER NOT HAVE TO WORRY ABOUT HIM. HE'S FINE ON HIS OWN BUT YOU HAVE A KEY. WOULD YOU BE ABLE TO PEEK IN ON HIM AND LET ME KNOW EVERYTHING'S OKAY? I'LL BE WITH SHERIFF PARKER FOR A WHILE—THERE'S BEEN ANOTHER MURDER—AND THEN I HAVE— I paused, feeling awkward. But finally, I shrugged and typed in, I HAVE A DATE WITH FARON.

As I locked the door, she texted back.

OF COURSE I CAN CHECK ON FANCYPANTS. LET ME KNOW WHEN YOU GET HOME. I'LL BE OVER IN ABOUT THIRTY MINUTES. She didn't say a word about Faron.

ARNIE FRYER WAS an excellent driver and—surprisingly—a funny man. On the way to the newest murder scene, he told me about his youngest daughter. Normally, I wasn't all that interested in stories about children, but apparently, he had a budding comedienne on his hands. I found my nerves calming as we approached a wooded thicket on the south side of town.

He sobered. "I have to warn you, they're still processing the scene, and the remains of the victim are still there. I hope you have a strong stomach. I recommend wearing a mask so you don't... It smells pretty rank." He motioned to the glove box. "There's a packet of masks in there. You should take one."

I pulled out one of the paper masks and slid the bands over my ears. My nerves were drumming a steady tattoo in the back of my mind and drops of cold sweat beaded on my forehead. As Arnie cautiously pulled onto the narrow access road, I tried to block out the memories that were cropping up unbidden of watching as the Butcher mutilated Rian.

And the rats...I hated rats as much as I hated vampires.

We pulled into a clearing where several of the sheriff's deputies' cars were parked. A group of people farther down the road were dressed in what looked like biohazard suits.

"Why are they wearing those suits?" I asked as Arnie brought the car to a stop.

"That's what I was talking about. The scene is gory, Elphyra. It looks like the killer went berserk, and the victim's remains are spread out over the area." He grimaced, shifting his gaze away as though he didn't want me to see the emotion that I could plainly hear in his voice.

"I see." I sat there for a moment, trying to build up my courage. I wasn't squeamish with a lot of things—and I had no problem with helping someone who had a cut or had hurt themselves. But a mutilated body was a long way from a skinned knee. Finally, I opened my door and stepped out of the car.

"Take me to the sheriff, please," I said.

Arnie silently led me down the road about twenty yards to where the sheriff was standing, mask on, watching silently as the coroner's team worked.

I glanced overhead. The sky was partially cloudy, and I could smell rain on the horizon. It would be here before evening. The afternoon seemed muted, and the forest had gone silent. The insects were still going about their day—bees gathering pollen, the sound of a few grasshoppers rustling in the bushes, but the birds were still, and there were no sounds of animals foraging through the woodland. I took a deep breath and reached out, trying to sense if there were any elementals or nature spirits but no one was willing to speak up, at least on the natural level.

Daisy glanced at me as we approached. She crooked her finger, motioning for me to follow. "Thank you for coming. It's pretty gruesome. With each murder, the killer seems to be devolving. He's losing more control with each victim. I'm actually glad Faron reached out to you. We could use your help, but I wasn't sure if you'd be all right with this, given"

"Given what happened to me?" I wasn't surprised she knew about Rian.

"Right."

"I'll do what I can," I said.

"I appreciate it." She paused, then added, "I assume that you know I checked out your background after what happened at Darla's house. I hope you aren't offended."

I shook my head. I would have too, given what we had found in the basement. "I get it," I said. Still, I felt exposed. My pain was a matter of public record.

"I'm sorry about what happened to you. Are you positive you can handle being here?" She sounded so earnest that I found any niggling doubts vanish.

"I'll manage. If something triggers me and I need to leave, I'll let you know."

I followed her down the road, Arnie at my side, trying to avert my eyes from the forensics team. But on the way, I caught sight as one of the men held up a partial hand. From where I stood, it looked like someone had taken a bite out of it. I looked away, counting to five before moving on.

"Faron says you're investigating Elroy, a member of his Pack," I said.

Daisy nodded. "The coroner insists that this resembles an alt-animal attack."

When a shifter turned into their animal form, they still had incredible strength—more so than the actual animal—and they still had their intelligence and awareness. In other words, they didn't lose themselves in the shift, though their perceptions were altered. So a shifter in animal form was called an alt-animal because they were capable of far more damage.

"But why assume it's a wolf shifter?"

"Unless they find DNA, and we *are* looking for it, we can't know for sure. But I do know that Elroy—since you know his name I'll use it—had beefs with both of the victims. He'd gotten in a fight with Lucius, and Olivia was suing him over some car accident. We have to investigate him."

I stopped, her words fading away. There, over near a tree, was the luminescent form of a man. He was leaning against the tree, watching the proceedings with a melancholy stare.

"I think I see the spirit of the victim. It was a man, right?"

"Right—his name was Jimithy Snare. He was—"

I gasped. "I know who Jimithy was."

He was famous among the witch clans. Demon hunters were specialized forms of witches, and Jimithy was one of the most famous. He'd taken down more monsters in a few short years than most people ever saw in a lifetime. The sheriff sounded tense, and she had a right to be. The demon hunters were integral to helping keep life on track for humans, shifters, and witches alike, and anybody capable of killing one had to be powerful.

"I thought you might," she said.

"I guarantee you, no *ordinary* wolf shifter could take Jimithy down. I'd look elsewhere than Faron's pack. I doubt if even Faron could take on Jimithy—"

But Daisy shook her head. "I *can't* look elsewhere. Not

yet. And I'm pretty sure that if I look, I'll find that Elroy had some beef with Jimithy as well. I can't write him off just because you think he wouldn't win against Jimithy in a cage match. Who's to say he didn't knock Jimithy out first? Or that he didn't use some kind of drug to get him out here? We can't assume anything until we have toxicology results."

"I understand," I argued, "but all I ask is that you be open to other possible suspects. Don't turn a blind eye toward other answers. There's absolutely no reason to limit yourself right now since you don't have any clear answers." In my desire to make certain that Daisy didn't make the dangerous move of overlooking other possibilities, I crossed the field to the ghost, motioning for the others to stay behind.

Hello, can you hear me? As I approached the spirit, I could see that it was, indeed, Jimithy. I'd met him once at a River's End Witch Clan meeting. My mother had taken me, my aunt, and my cousin. It had been years ago, when I was in my early teens, but even then, Jimithy had made a name for himself.

Yes. You look familiar. You're a witch, aren't you? What element are you bound to? The ghost was wearing a black leather jacket, a pair of jeans, and a polo shirt.

I wondered if that was what he'd been wearing when he died, but I wasn't going to go look through the body parts to find out. *I'm bound to the earth and water. Hey, we met when I was young. It was at a Gathering of the Clans. I was twelve and part of the River's End Witch Clan.*

Ah...the 2001 gathering that was held down in Centralia?

That's the one. Anyway, I... I wasn't sure what to say. Was it proper to offer sympathy to a ghost for dying? There were so many social niceties that weren't covered in the usual magical textbooks. *I have some questions for the sheriff. Do you mind answering?*

Ask away. Jimithy shifted against the tree. His spirit was glowing, illuminated by a nimbus so bright he was hard to look at.

First and foremost: do you know who killed you? I held my breath, praying he wouldn't say it was Elroy.

Not exactly. I was minding my own business, taking a run on one of the trails in this thicket. It's part of Alimara Park, you know. Next thing I know, some guy's jogging past me in the opposite direction. Wolf shifter, by the scent. But there was something about him that set off my alarms, so I stopped. When I turned around to get a better look at him, I realized that he had stopped shortly after passing me and he was right on my heels. I had no warning—there was no noise, no intuition other than the vague feeling that the man was questionable.

How did he take you down? I asked.

He had a mallet—it was small but heavy enough that when he took a swing at me, he managed to knock me unconscious. I have no clue what it's made out of, but all it took was one hit. I woke up in the middle of...he was ripping my guts out of me. I managed to register what was happening, but that's all. The next moment, I passed out, and when I opened my eyes, I was here—dead.

I nodded. This was all useful information, though the part about the wolf shifter was going to complicate matters.

Do you know who the shifter was? Better ask now and get it over with.

No, I don't, other than it was a man—or an exceptionally strong woman in drag. But I sensed "male"... And he didn't feel like he was from "here," if you know what I mean. He felt other*—almost alien. But I can tell you for sure, it was a wolf shifter.*

That didn't help my case at all, but I would tell the sheriff because—if it was Elroy—we needed to know. But Faron wasn't going to be happy.

Is there anything you'd like me to tell your family?

He was starting to fade. Spirits like Jimithy—who were so strong in energy—either crossed through the Veil without hesitation, or they stuck around and made major nuisances of themselves. Luckily for us, Jimithy didn't seem inclined to stay.

Please tell my wife I loved her, and that I would give anything to be able to stay with her and my boys. And tell my sons that... Tell them their daddy will always watch out for them. Don't tell them I suffered. Reassure them that I went quick—that's the least I can do for Shawna and the kids.

As he faded out of sight, I felt an intense, almost painful longing, but then it diffused into the air around me and he was gone. I turned back to Daisy, dreading telling her the truth. But I was honest, and just because he said a wolf shifter killed him, didn't mean it was Elroy.

"Did you see him?" she asked.

I nodded. "Yeah, we talked. First, he wants you to tell his wife that he didn't suffer. That's a lie, of course, but it's for their sake more than anything. He wants her and their boys to know how much he loves them and that he'll be watching over them."

"He *did* suffer," she started to say but then stopped. "I get it. Okay. Did he say anything about who killed him?"

I nodded. "Yeah, but please—don't jump to conclusions."

"What do you mean?" She paused. "A wolf shifter killed him, am I right?"

Sighing, I said, "Yes, but he couldn't identify who it was." I hastened to add, "Please, don't assume it was Elroy."

"Have you *met* Elroy?" Daisy asked.

I shook my head. "No, I haven't."

"Then you haven't formed an opinion about him," Daisy said. "I'll tell you what. You meet him, and then you come back and tell me you're championing him and I might take it more seriously. But mark my words. Elroy Zastratha is trouble. He's been in and out of jail for the past two decades. He's become increasingly erratic. I know Faron wants to protect him, but the truth is, Elroy needs professional help. And it goes beyond getting in trouble."

I caught something behind her words. "What do you mean?"

"I mean...Elroy is a troubled man, and I'm not just talking about legal issues. At the least, I think he needs a good psychiatrist. If it's as bad as I think, he needs to be locked away and watched over." She glanced around. "All right, I think you're done here. Why don't you and Arnie check out the other murder sites?"

"All right." I turned to go, thinking that she was right. I hadn't met Elroy and I was basing my opinion on someone who I wasn't sure I could trust. As I headed over to Arnie, Daisy called out behind me.

"Elphyra?"

"Yes?" I turned.

"Be careful if you decide to meet Elroy. Remember what I said."

As Arnie escorted me back to his car, I thought about Jimithy. Demon hunters were astute—they were the strongest of witches. There was no doubt in my mind that he meant what he said. He had been killed by a wolf shifter, and how was I going to break the news to Faron?

CHAPTER FOURTEEN

After I visited the other two sites, on the way back to my place, Daisy called. I answered as Arnie drove sedately along Oak Leaf Road, the road that I lived on. I gazed out the window as the early evening shadows fell.

"Hey, what's up?" I asked.

Daisy wasted no time. "I forgot to ask you to please keep what you learned quiet. I'd prefer it if you don't tell Faron what you found out this afternoon. And what happened with the two other murder sites? Were Olivia or Lucius's spirits still hanging around?"

"No. I didn't pick up on anything there, except the strong sense of sadness and fear that always permeates tragic surroundings." I frowned. "Why don't you want me telling Faron what Jimithy told me?"

"Think about it: he's desperately trying to protect one of his own. Now, I am not saying that I'm headed over to lock up Elroy—we don't have enough evidence. But if Faron knows that Jimithy bore out our suspicion about a wolf shifter, he might try to protect Elroy by hiding him. Consider this privileged police information. We always hold things back in investigations that only the killer might know." She was silent for a moment, and it hit me that she was waiting for my response. I couldn't very well refuse.

"All right, I promise. Though he's so worried—"

"Faron Collinsworth will manage until we're further along in our investigation. What worries me now, though, is how do I approach the town about this. With a third murder, I *have* to say something. It's obvious we have some sort of serial killer on the loose, and people need to be on the alert. I suppose I'll have to call Nan and ask her to put me on the local news before people start marching outside my office, protesting that I'm not doing my job."

"Who's Nan?"

"She runs the programming for the Dabob Bay News, an online news site that airs every evening, streaming. I can't take a chance by not warning people. If we had someone else show up dead, and I hadn't put out a warning, there would be hell to pay."

Daisy sounded so depressed that I wanted to cheer her up, but I couldn't think of anything to say that would work. "All right. I promise to keep quiet."

"Thank you. I have to go. I have reports to finish, and the coroner needs to wrap up things out here." She sighed. "What a waste. I hate cleaning up after murders. Such sense-less violence."

I slid my phone back in its case, which was strapped around my arm. As I leaned back, staring out the window, the immensity of dealing with cases like this struck me.

"Do you ever get tired of your job?" I asked Arnie.

He shrugged. "I think everybody does at some time in their life. I'm pretty sure every cop, at one point or another, wishes he didn't have to face the darker sides of the world. But almost all of us want to make a difference—to help people in some way. And this happens to be the way we contribute. Oh, there are bad cops. I won't deny that. But for the most part, we just want to protect people."

"Witches are, by nature, given to walk in the shadow side. But it's hard for me...now. I used to be able to without blinking, but things change when those shadows hit you in the gut." I shook my head. "I swore when I left Port Townsend that I wouldn't get involved again. That I'd focus my life on growing things, on life instead of death. And here I am—again—steeped in the underworld." I shifted in my seat. "Do you think it's ever possible to leave it behind?"

Arnie didn't answer for a moment. Then he said, "I don't know. For someone like me, I can walk away from the job, but I'll never forget what I've seen. But when it's in your blood, like you? I'd like to think that you can escape your destiny, but I'm not at all certain." He pulled into my driveway and drove up the graveled path. "Here we are—you're home, safe and sound."

As I stepped out of the car, I leaned down. "Thanks, Arnie. For the company, as well as the ride. I'll see you later. Take care. Be safe."

He saluted me, but before he pulled out again, said, "Maybe focus on the good you do, rather than the toll it takes? That might help."

I waved as he turned in the loop and then headed back toward the graveled road. Maybe he was right. Maybe that was exactly what I needed to do.

FANCYPANTS WAS CURLED UP ASLEEP on the sofa when I entered the living room. May had left a note telling me that everything looked good, that he'd eaten a good dinner, and that she'd be back around nine to check on things. I decided to let him sleep and went into the bedroom to dress for my date. The afternoon had put a decided damper on my mood, but what weighed on me more heavily than anything was: what was I going to tell Faron? I'd done as he requested, but now I couldn't tell him what I'd found out.

It was seven, so I had an hour till he showed up. I decided a shower was in order, and dinner required more than jeans and a shirt. I slid out of my clothes and stepped into the spray of water. I was lathering up and my mind was starting to drift as the knots of the day worked themselves out of my shoulders when the shower curtain rustled.

I let out a shriek. Abruptly, the curtain ripped away from the rings and Fancypants, caught in the swirl of material, crashed to the floor. Luckily, the material softened his fall.

I stood there, buck naked as the shower spray continued to spew hot water, as the dragonette sputtered and tried to worm his way out of the tangle of cloth.

"What the hell were you doing? You scared the crap out of me!" I turned off the faucet and grabbed for a towel, wrapping it around myself.

"Hey, I'm no peeping Tom!" Fancypants managed to extricate himself from the shower curtain. He fluttered each wing, testing them to make certain they weren't broken.

"Why did you sneak up on me like that?" Shaking, I stepped out of my shower and sat down on the vanity stool. My hair was still frothing from the shampoo and I had soap scum—or what would soon turn into soap scum—all over my body.

"I didn't mean to! I was coming in to say hello." He landed on the vanity counter near me. "I'm sorry. I didn't mean to startle you."

"I know," I said. "But I'm skittish right now. Please, announce yourself before scaring the shit out of me." I stretched, yawning. Right now, I didn't feel like going out with Faron. Right now, the only thing I wanted to do was curl up in my bed and rest.

"I'll let you finish showering," Fancypants said. He flew up and out of the bathroom.

"Thank you." I didn't want to make him feel bad, but right now wasn't a good time to startle me. I stepped back into the shower and turned the water on again, rinsing my hair and washing the soap off my skin.

As I dried my hair and put a fresh face of makeup on, I decided on my outfit. I'd wear a short black tank dress over a pair of green and white striped leggings. I chose a thin gold belt—I couldn't remember if shifters liked silver or hated it—and paired the outfit with a leaf-green cardigan that matched the leggings. I exchanged my platform boots for a pair of ballerina flats and then transferred my wallet, keys, and phone into a clutch. I dried my hair and brushed it out so that it flowed down my shoulders. As a final touch, I added the smoky quartz pendant and gold hoop earrings. Then, standing back, I stared at myself in the mirror.

It had been so long since I looked at myself in this way—as a woman, rather than just as a reflection of someone I used to be. My tattoos, full sleeves from just above the elbow down to my wrists, were vibrant and bright.

I met my eyes in the mirror.

"You can do this," I said to myself. "You can manage one date. You're not betraying Rian's memory. He'd want you to be happy."

As I mouthed the words so many people had said to me over the past year, I could *almost* believe them. Rian was the most caring, generous man I'd ever met. He never had a bad word for anybody unless they came for me. He treated me like a queen. And *he* would want me to be happy—he never begrudged joy.

"I miss you," I said, whispering to the image in my mind.

"I miss your touch. I miss your smile. I miss the future we planned. I miss...my life—and your life."

And then, something happened that had never happened before. Rian walked out of the shadows of my thoughts, into the light to stand in front of me. I reached out, and to my surprise, I felt his energy. This was no hallucination.

"Rian?" I asked, breathless. "Is that really you?"

Out of all the ghosts and spirits I'd seen since I lost him, Rian had never once been among them. Whether it was my keen sense of loss or the pain of remembering how he died that prevented him from visiting, I didn't know. But he'd never before come to me except in painful dreams where he was still alive and we were still happy together.

It's me, my love. Oh, Elphyra, I'm so sorry I had to leave you along the way. His voice was exactly as I remembered it, and it hit me in the gut.

"I *miss* you," I said, sinking to my knees in front of him. "I miss everything about our life together." I wanted to bury my head in my hands and weep, but I couldn't take my eyes away from him, not now that he was here in front of me again. I knew he was only here in spirit, but to have him near meant everything in the world.

I miss you too. But you have to let me go, Elf. You have to let me move on. I can't leave because you're holding me so tight. I don't want to leave you, but I can't linger, either. It's not healthy. You have to let go of the guilt. It wasn't your fault. You weren't *the reason I died.* He knelt beside me, his arm out as though he was about to take my hand. I wanted to reach for it but knew that my hand would go right through his.

"How can I let go? You're all I have—"

No, I'm not. You have so much in your life, and so many things to do. You stepped off of the web and into the shadows when I died. You've been living a half-life. You have a world left to explore, a life to live. I had to leave earlier than we planned, but I don't want you to stop living for me. *What kind of person would I be if I wanted you to exist in sorrow?* He reached out to stroke my hair and I could almost feel his hand on my face.

"How do I *do* that? How do I let you go? I'll have to face the world alone again." I did reach for him at that point, but as I had feared, my hand went through his and it hit me—he was getting ready to leave me for good. I was going to be all alone.

You aren't *alone, love. You have friends. Fancypants will be there for you when all else is dark and empty. And May, she's the grand- mother you always wanted. And Bree—she has your back. You still have your family. I've been watching out for you and I've wanted to talk to you so many times, but there was no way through the bubble of pain you erected around yourself.*

"Will we ever meet again?" I asked, tears tracing their way down my cheeks. "I can't imagine never seeing you again."

I'll check in on you now and then. And yes, someday in the future, when it's time, I'll be waiting for you and we can decide what to do from there. We're not done. We have a bond between us that isn't ready to break. But you have to let me move on until then. And you have to grow and live and learn what you need to learn.

His voice was beginning to fade.

I dashed my tears away, trying to be strong for him. "I won't ever love anybody else—"

You will. And you'll take joy in it. And I'll be happy for you. What you create with someone else doesn't eliminate the love we had. We had a beautiful bond. And we'll have that again, sometime long in the future. But love isn't finite. You can love someone else, without destroying what we shared. I want you to promise me that you'll stop hiding from the world. You'll go out there and take it by the horns and show it who's boss. You'll drive your life, instead of letting it run over you. Do you promise me this, on your sacred oath?

He leaned close and I could feel him now—that warm, intense energy left me breathless. How could I say no? How could I leave him worrying about me when he was at the crossroads, ready to walk into a different world?

"I'll... I'll try. I'll do my best. But it won't be easy," I said.

Nobody ever said life was easy—or fair. Sometimes, we get handed the short stick and we have to make the best of it. If we waited for everything to be in perfect alignment, we'd be waiting forever. Go out there and make the life you want, for me—and for you.

I nodded. I'd heard this all before, but coming from Rian, it made a huge difference. He was giving me permission to walk ahead into the future without him. And that was the one piece that had been missing. I felt so guilty about leaving him behind that I hadn't been able to do anything at all. Now, he was kicking me out of the nest. I was a fledgling again, and he had decided that it was time I learn to fly all over again.

"I will," I said. "I give you my word, I'll make you proud. And when it comes time, I'll watch for you."

And when it's time, I'll be there, waiting for you. Now, go. Have fun. Live life. Be free.

As he blew me a kiss and I caught it, he faded out of sight. And then he was gone. And I felt truly alone.

CHAPTER FIFTEEN

At precisely eight p.m., Faron arrived. Fancypants retreated to the bedroom as I opened the door. Faron stood there, staring at me. He wore a pair of black jeans, a form-fitting button-down blue shirt that was open to the second button. His hair was pulled back in a long, sleek ponytail, and he was wearing motorcycle boots. His eyes glittered as he held out a bouquet of red roses.

"I figured, after the other day, I couldn't go wrong with flowers," he said, shifting uncertainly to his other foot.

"Thank you," I said, taken aback. "Let me put these in water before we go."

I invited him in while I went into the kitchen and found a vase. I would cut the stems later. I filled the vase with water and set the flowers on the counter.

"I'm glad you like them," Faron said, startling me. He was behind me, leaning in so his hands were on the counter on each side of me. His face was near my neck and I could feel his breath. I started to panic.

"Get away from my neck!" I half-turned, shoving him back.

He stumbled, looking startled. "I'm sorry," he said, holding up his hands. "I wasn't going to attack you, I promise!"

I wrapped my arms around me, images of the Butcher running through my mind. He had been standing behind Rian, his fangs buried in Rian's neck. I tried to clear my head.

Damn it, the vamp's curse made every memory feel like it had happened yesterday. My mind knew that it had been over a year, but inside, the images were too vivid, too clear. I could once again hear the sound of the vampire sucking, I could hear Rian's moan—the Butcher made his assaults passionate at first, before turning up the fear and the pain.

Faron stared at me, worry filling his face. "Are you all right? Elphyra—I'm so sorry. I didn't mean to scare you."

I shook my head. "No, you...I know you didn't." I forced the panic down, counting from one to ten. Then I reached out and started tapping on the side of my left hand with my right index and middle fingers. I breathed through the fear as Faron watched, and after a moment, I let out a long breath and relaxed.

"I'm sorry about that. I would have warned you that I have PTSD, but I didn't think..."

"That I would intrude on your space like that," he said. "I'm so sorry. That was inappropriate. I won't ask what happened to bring that on, but if you ever want to tell me, I'll listen. I didn't think," he added, holding me with his gaze. "Again, I apologize."

"I told you, it's okay." I stared at him back, well aware that for wolves the move was a challenge. But I wasn't going to look away. I wasn't going to be the one to break contact because I wasn't the one in the wrong.

He paused for a moment, then said, "Do you still feel like going to dinner? I'll understand if you say no—"

"Do you still *want* to go out with me after..." I stopped.

Then, taking a fresh breath, I said, "Faron, I come with a fuckton of baggage. I haven't dated anybody in over a year—and I have my reasons. I don't want you to get the wrong idea. I'm not looking for a relationship. I'm not looking...for anything except peace of mind." I shrugged, feeling resigned. Resigned to what, I wasn't sure, but this had shown me that I wasn't healed. I might never heal. And I had to get used to that idea.

I couldn't read the look on his face, but he straightened and smiled. "I'd still like to have dinner with you, if you're willing."

Feeling oddly relieved, I nodded. "All right, then. Let's go." Grabbing my purse, I led him to the door and locked it as we exited. I wasn't sure what to expect, but I felt like I'd at least made a little progress by keeping the date.

THE DRIVE to Bianca's Bistro took all of ten minutes—it was at the center of town—and during that time neither one of us said anything. I was trying to process what had happened and whether I should tell Faron my background, but by the time we pulled into a pay parking lot not far from Bianca's, I was no closer to an answer.

We parked a block from the restaurant, as close as we could get, and Faron hurried around the car to open my door for me. We walked in silence to the restaurant. The hostess led us to a booth and I slid in on one side, Faron on the other. She took our drink orders—Faron asked for scotch on the rocks, and I ordered a lemon daiquiri. Leaving a basket of breadsticks on the table, she left us with menus as she headed back to the bar.

"So, how is Starlight Hollow treating you?" Faron asked.

I stared at him for a moment, then—not wanting to play

the small-talk game—said, "I'll tell you why I reacted like that. You deserve an explanation."

"You don't have to—" he started.

I shook my head. "No, but I want to. If you're going to be in my life at all, you need to know this. I warn you, it isn't pleasant. In fact, it's pretty gruesome, so if you want I can wait until after dinner." I paused as the waitress brought our drinks.

When she was gone, Faron said, "Go ahead. I've seen a wide spectrum of things in this lifetime and they haven't been all pleasant."

So I told him. He didn't interrupt me as I laid out what had happened, and how the Butcher still had cords latched into me. "May is going to help me get rid of those attachments on Saturday. Hopefully, that will prevent him from tracking me down later. And maybe, just maybe, that will break the hold he has on me so that every time I think about Rian's death, it doesn't feel like it happened yesterday."

Faron had sat silent throughout my story, his expression growing somber as his eyes widened. After I finished, he continued to sit there, drink in hand. He swallowed, hard, and finally said, "I'm so incredibly sorry. I don't know what to say."

"There isn't much you can say. There aren't any Hallmark cards for 'Sorry your fiancé was butchered in front of you and you had to watch the rats begin to devour his body.' " I stopped, wincing. "I'm sorry again—I'm bitter, I know. I try not to take it out on others, but sometimes it's so hard." I flashed back to Rian's ghostly visit and added, "I'm trying to move on, but it hurts. I know he wants me to live, to grow and thrive, but it feels like I'm leaving him behind."

"Survivor's guilt," Faron said, sliding his hand across the table, palm open and facing up. He waited.

I stared at his fingers, then quietly placed my hand in his.

His hands were so large compared to mine. I had long narrow fingers, but his hands were large and callused. I could feel his feral blood beating in his veins. I could almost smell the musky scent that followed him.

"You aren't leaving him behind," Faron said. "He'll always be with you. He'll always be in your heart. You can't ever lose the love you had with him. He died. It wasn't his fault. It wasn't yours. You were both in the wrong place at the wrong time, and the only blame there is on the vampire who did this to you."

"Everybody tells me to get over it, that it's time to move on...I know, logically, that I can't let myself get mired but sometimes, the chasm feels so deep that I have to look up to see the bottom." My voice was thick with tears. "I don't want to say goodbye, Faron. I don't want to see him leave my life. His spirit is moving on—he came to me earlier today for the first time and we talked. He's ready to move on and asked me to let go. But how..."

"How do you do that?" Faron asked. "It's not easy. It requires sacrifice. Let go because it's best for them—not for you. You move on because it's a selfless act and it sets their spirit free. You go through the motions at first, and after a while, the motions become real, and you find yourself invested in life again."

I caught a glimpse of something in his eyes. Something that told me he understood me on a visceral level. That he'd been through what I was facing.

"What happened to you?" I asked, my voice soft.

"I lost my wife, ten years ago," he said.

At that moment, the server appeared to take our order.

I let go of his hand and cleared my throat. "I'd like fried calamari for an appetizer, and then the fettucine Alfredo."

Faron ordered the chicken Parmesan, and for an appetizer, he asked for a tomato-basil salad. "We can share appetizers if you like," he said.

"That sounds good."

The waitress took our orders and left us alone. Her interruption had given me enough time to breathe and take a step back so that I wasn't on the verge of tears.

After she was gone, Faron cleared his throat. "I was married for ten years to a woman named Giada. She was a true Alpha among the women, and we were a power couple. She was far from a trophy wife, though she *was* beautiful. She ran an insurance company. We fell for each other instantly, and our families approved the match. So we married. We wanted kids, we planned on big family get-togethers. She was beloved by the entire Pack."

"What happened? Do you have any children?" I asked.

He shook his head. "No, we thought we had time so we decided to wait to establish a family until we could pay off our debts. We wanted to see the world—to travel back to Italy. Her family was Italian. Mine is British. A month led into a year led into a decade. We bought our dream home, and the Pack was thriving thanks to our leadership."

"You sound like you were made for each other," I murmured. "Soulmates?"

"Not exactly, but...yes, we complemented each other. Anyway, we finally decided to start a family and Giada told me she was pregnant. She had this glow to her—she was radiant."

A light filled his eyes, and though I had never seen her, I could feel how beautiful she had been. I kept quiet, waiting for him to proceed at his own pace.

"It was near Samhain, ten years ago this year. The holiday has always made me nervous. In our Pack, we tend to see it as the time when—if you're going to die in the next year—the gods mark you on that night. We bought candy for the secular kids for Halloween, and we handed it out. Well, around seven-thirty, the doorbell rang. Giada answered, but there was nobody there, Yet it felt like something had entered the house. Both she and I noticed it."

"A ghost, perhaps? The spirits walk on Samhain," I said.

"Yes, they do, but this felt deeper—like something powerful had walked over the threshold. It was as though a shadow had entered our lives. We didn't talk about it over the next week or so, but in mid-November, Giada had to visit a potential client who lived over on the shores of Lake Crescent."

Lake Crescent was a lake on Highway 101, near the Strait of Juan de Fuca. Known for swallowing people at will, the lake was dark and deep, and the roads alongside it were dangerous in the autumn and winter months. All it took was one wrong shift of the wheel and the icy depths waited with hunger. There was a creature in the lake, it was reputed, and the Lady of Lake Crescent was a well-known spirit.

A woman had been murdered and dumped in the lake in the late 1930s. She had been reported as missing, but some years later, her body appeared. She'd been saponified—essentially turned into a bar of soap by the chemicals inherent within the lake. Her husband was convicted of murder. Her spirit roamed the shores of the lake, it was thought, and she called people to her when she was lonely.

"Crescent Lake is a wild, dangerous area," I said.

"It is. And during inclement weather, it's worse. I begged her not to go. It was too dangerous—the roads are never good that time of year. But if she could contract this client, it would mean a huge coup. She had the chance to earn a five-figure commission and more work, given the scope of the policies he was interested in. So she kissed me goodbye and promised to take it easy. She left the house at eight-ten. I remember glancing at my watch and thinking I was late for work." His voice was thick now, as he stared into his drink.

I waited, not wanting to hear the end, but he had listened to me, and now I would listen to him. The world was so dark sometimes that all I craved were bright lights and sparkles.

"Two hours later, Kent—the sheriff here before Daisy—showed up on my doorstep with the news. The wind had knocked a tree over onto Highway 101, right around a bend in the road. Giada didn't know about it, it had just happened, so nobody had a chance to report it and set up roadblocks. She rounded the curve at fifty miles per hour. She saw the tree too late, and in trying to avoid running headlong into it, she put on the brakes and skidded to the side. Her car went through the guard railing, into the lake. She drowned, and our baby with her, too. They found her around half an hour after the accident, from what I gather. In a single moment, I lost my wife, baby, and the future that we had been heading toward."

He looked up at me and I could sense the pain in his voice. I reached out this time, palm open and facing up, and he took my fingers. I squeezed tight, holding him as the memories worked their way across his face.

"I'm sorry," I said. "I'm sorry about both Giada and your child."

He squeezed my fingers. "Thank you. I didn't have to watch her drown, but I could feel her panic. In the Pack, we're connected, though it's strongest between mated pairs. I knew something was wrong. I didn't know what, but I knew it was bad. I texted her every ten minutes with no answer." He paused, then added, "My last text was angry. I accused her of ignoring me. I pray she never saw it."

"She didn't," I said. "I can feel it in my gut." I paused as the waitress brought our appetizers. She left and then—before he had a chance to pull back, I gave his fingers another squeeze. "We're both the victims of fate—tragedy, if you like."

Our sharing of secrets had formed an odd bond. It felt like we were members of an exclusive club, one that I'd rather never be part of, but it bonded us together. I wanted to ask several questions: How did he move on? How had he let go of the past? Had he ever felt to blame, and what had he done about it? But it wasn't the right time to question him.

I lifted my glass. "Here's to the past—to the people we loved. To the people who made our lives feel whole."

He joined me, lifting his glass, but all the while, he never let go of my gaze and there were a million questions he seemed to be asking. We drank our toast, and the waitress brought our dinners. By the time we were ready to eat, the moment had passed, and we moved on to a lighter part of the date—the getting-to-know-you topics like what your favorite foods were, what kind of movies did you like, and so forth.

The evening proceeded and we left the topics of our losses untouched. It felt as though, by touching the dark, we had opened up a way to walk in the light. I knew that, if we were to continue dating, the discussion would have to come up again, but for now, I wanted to enjoy the breathing space.

To sit with a man in a restaurant without crying, letting the past be in the past for even an hour, gave me grace and a reprieve. For a while, I could pretend—and so could he. And so we ate and drank, and talked about the town and our lives, all the while keeping room between us and the edge of the chasm.

CHAPTER SIXTEEN

Near the end of dinner, which had been surprisingly pleasant once we moved onto other topics, Faron cleared his throat and looked up from his crème brûlée. "Would you like to meet Elroy? I shouldn't expect you to believe me about him until you've had a chance to meet him."

I wasn't sure how much more energy I could handle, but it seemed a fair request. I wavered. Given what Daisy had told me about him, this would be a chance to either put my suspicions to rest or to decide that I couldn't believe in his innocence.

"Sure. Where do we have to go?"

"Usually, I'd have to take you out on the communal land, but he happens to be working tonight. He's an architect. So we have to save it for another day."

I must have looked startled because Faron gave me the side-eye. "What? Wolf shifters can't be architects?"

"That's not what I was thinking," I said. "It's...the way you described him, and the way that Daisy described him, I would have pegged him for a dockhand or something."

"You can have a temper and still be smart," Faron said.

I nodded. "I know. So what's he doing working this late?"

"His firm is on the clock for a project that was supposed to be finished a couple weeks ago. They're scrambling, trying to finish now. It's the client's fault—he kept changing his mind and then changing it back after they revised the plans. I'm not sure what the project is, but I know Elroy and his partner, Wilson, have been neck-deep trying to keep up with the requests." Faron pushed back his plate. He glanced at mine—I'd stopped a few bits short of finishing my pie. "If you're done, we can have them wrap up the rest of that to go with your steak."

I'd only managed to eat half my steak, so had asked the server to wrap the rest to go. I figured Fancypants might like it, and if he didn't, I could slice it thin and make a sandwich out of it.

"I'm good," I said, taking one last bite. "Dinner was wonderful, but I don't have much of an appetite tonight."

I didn't want him to think I hadn't enjoyed myself, though I wasn't exactly sure if I had. But Faron had been polite, and I was surprised by how open he had been about his losses and his life. Plus, I found myself staring into those gorgeous eyes, falling into their coffee-dark light. It was hard to look away, and it was hard to admit that I was attracted to the man.

He motioned for the check and when the waitress handed it to him, he placed his credit card in the leather check holder. The server gave him a faint nod and, after asking if everything had been acceptable, left.

"Thank you for tonight," Faron said.

"I'm glad you asked," I said, pushing back my chair as we waited for the check to come back. When the waitress appeared, he glanced at the total, wrote in a tip, then signed the slip. The waitress returned his card to him and we stood, weaving through the tables on our way to the door. As we ventured into the cool night air, I found myself imagining him taking me in hand, pulling me to him for a kiss, slipping his hand under my shirt. As I shivered, he escorted me into the night and we headed for the car.

DOWNTOWN STARLIGHT HOLLOW was a lovely place at night. With most of the crowds out of the way, only a few wayward souls straggled through the city streets, most in search of the next bar, and even the drunks were reasonably pleasant.

Still, as we walked back to the car, I slid closer to Faron, nervous about being out at night, especially after we'd had a couple of drinks.

But this isn't Port Townsend. What happened to you was one in a million. It won't happen again. You can't spend your life jumping at shadows, can you?

I tried to ignore the voice, but I couldn't. I took a deep breath and stepped away from his side, glancing around me as I tried to unbiasedly analyze the energy in the streets tonight.

"You okay?" he asked.

I nodded. "I'm okay. Yes. I'm trying out a piece of advice that Rian gave me when he visited me. I'm trying to return to the land of the living."

"It can take time," Faron said. "I told you that it took me a couple years, but I managed it. But I never drive that road in the winter—ever. I can't, especially since the area where she died is so clear in my mind."

"Just like I'll never walk the streets of Port Townsend again, not at night. I have to admit, I'm nervous. I don't usually go out at night."

"You're with me, I won't let anything happen to you," Faron said.

I gave him a long look. "Rian thought he was immune to

danger, too." I didn't want to see Faron as trouble. He was too nice—nicer than I ever thought possible. And he was cute. There was something about him that made me want to lean in close, to stare into his eyes. *No...it was more than that.* There was something about him that made me want to get to *know* him.

"I think I'd better be getting home," I said as we reached the car.

He was silent for a moment, then opened my door and I slid in and fastened my seat belt, too aware of the energy between us. The tension was thick as we drove back to my house, but the minute we reached the driveway, I thanked him and opened the door.

"You don't have to get out—but I'd appreciate it if you'd keep watch to make sure I get inside," I said.

He nodded. "I won't stay, but I'm walking you to the door and waiting for the all-clear once you get inside." And that was what he did. He didn't try for a kiss, he didn't take my hand, but at the door he refused to leave until I went inside, peeked through the house, and made certain everything was in order.

"Everything's fine," I said, returning to the door. I felt like a heel, but I was so overwhelmed by the evening that I didn't trust myself not to jump into something I wasn't ready for yet. "Thank you again. I enjoyed the evening." Everything coming out of my mouth sounded so cool and aloof that I was desperate to shut the door and decompress.

"Then, I'll see you later. I had a wonderful time as well. Thank you for your help," he added. "I wish that Elroy was in the clear."

"I do too," I said, shutting the door and locking it. And I realized that I meant it.

NEXT MORNING, Fancypants woke me up by flapping his wings in my face. Murky images filled my dreams, and I felt vaguely uneasy. I attributed it to the dinner with Faron, and as I fed the dragonette, I tried to put the evening behind me. It wasn't my problem that the cops suspected Elroy. Faron *had* been the one to ask me if I could contact the ghosts of the victims. That Jimithy had told me a wolf shifter killed him wasn't my fault. It had been a calculated risk that Faron took and it had played out the wrong way.

I looked at Fancypants as he was inhaling his breakfast. "I know you're only a few days old, but how did you learn to speak English from a few hours of bonding?"

He paused, looking up from the plate of sausage and eggs on the counter. "Well, it's like sleep learning, in a sense. The brain is far more complex than most people realize. Dragons can learn at an incredible rate, and in our sleep, our cognition processes are even faster. So once the bond was first made, and that was when I was in the egg, I absorbed the knowledge from you. I don't have your *memories,* but rather the actual knowledge of how to communicate. And we're graced with a species memory that we're born with."

"Well, that's handy," I said, toying with my own breakfast, which was the same thing Fancypants was eating. I sighed.

"What's wrong?" Fancypants asked.

"I feel bad about abruptly ending my date last night. I went from hot to cold, and I don't know if Faron understood why I suddenly pulled back. I also feel like the two things I did this week to try to help people out, I failed at. All I did was stir up things with—" I paused as my phone rang. A glance at the screen told me it was Daisy. "Hello?"

"Hey, Elphyra, I wanted to tell you that the coroner couldn't find a cause of death on the skeletons. While it's unlikely they died of natural causes, we can't be sure. We do know they didn't put themselves in that basement. Anyway, we're releasing the objects from the trunk to Darla today, and the remains are going to be buried in Hatfield Cemetery this afternoon."

I thought for a moment. "Can I attend the burial and salt the bones before they go in the ground? Would that be considered desecrating the bodies?"

Daisy paused, then said, "I think I can look the other way. Will that work?"

"If Darla lets me at those items that were in the trunk, and I can salt the bones as well, it should end the haunting and that should also help bring her husband back to his senses." My spirits lifted—at least there was hope.

"Meet me at the cemetery at two P.M. I'll be there in case the gravediggers decide to protest. By the way, we checked back through all the records and can't figure out who they were. Dental records led nowhere. It looks like they were old when they died, and we've talked to everybody we can find who was associated with that house and nobody claims any knowledge of them. But there are a few families we can't trace, who either rented or owned the house during the past fifty years."

I felt vaguely disappointed—I really wanted to know who the old women were—but at least Darla would have her house back. "I'll meet you at two. Oh, did you make any headway on the murders?"

"We brought in Elroy for questioning. He's passed a lie detector test, but that doesn't fully prove his innocence. I did a spot on the news last night, warning people to be cautious. Now let's hope that we catch this freak before he murders anybody else."

She said goodbye and I set my phone back on the table.

"Good news?" Fancypants asked. "You look relieved."

"Well, on one front, yes. I guess sometimes we have to accept the wins the way they come to us and let go of the losses." I finished my breakfast as a text from Bree came through.

LEAVING TODAY ON A TRIP UP TO HURRICANE RIDGE. I'LL BE BACK SUNDAY AFTERNOON. HOW ARE YOU? WHAT'S GOING ON? TEXT ME. I MAY NOT BE ABLE TO GET BACK TO YOU RIGHT AWAY, BUT I WANT TO KNOW THAT YOU AND YOUR DRAGONETTE ARE OKAY.

I texted her back. I'LL BE ABLE TO SALT THE BONES OF THOSE TWO OLD BIDDIES TODAY THANKS TO DAISY, SO ONE PROBLEM TAKEN CARE OF. BE CAREFUL—I KNOW YOU WILL BUT HURRICANE RIDGE CAN BE DANGEROUS, EVEN IN SUMMER. HAVE FUN!

At that moment, a knock on the kitchen door startled me. I answered to find Bran standing there. "Hey, come on in. What brings you over?"

He was carrying a basket covered with a tea towel. It smelled incredible. "I thought I'd come work some more on your driveway. My mother sent you goodies." He handed me the basket and, as I took it, he noticed the roses on the counter. "Pretty. From your bushes?"

Bran knew perfectly well that my rose bushes weren't in bloom yet. "No. Faron gave them to me."

"That's right, your *big date*," Bran said, a touch too casually. "Have fun?"

I peeked under the tea towel. A loaf of bread, four blueberry muffins, and some homemade butter and a jar of preserves. "Yum, this looks wonderful. I'll text her a thank-you."

I wasn't going to take the bait, but I glanced at Bran, and once again, I felt that sudden aura of calmness around him. It hit me in all the feels and I realized that I trusted him. I trusted him more than I'd trusted anybody in a long time, and I couldn't pinpoint why.

"Faron was a gentleman," I said, cautiously. "We went to

dinner." I stacked the breakfast dishes in the sink and finished off my latte.

I didn't want to stir up the obvious rivalry they had—and I guessed that it went far beyond friendship with me. The two must have been at odds for quite a while, which wasn't all that surprising given Faron was a wolf shifter and Bran a witch. I'd been surprised that the date actually happened, let alone turned out well, for the same reason.

"I'm going to spend some time in the workshop this morning, creating some spell kits for the shop. If you need me, that's where I'll be." I turned to Fancypants. "You want to come with me?"

"Maybe. I'll take a nap first, though." Fancypants had finished his breakfast and yawned. He burped, then flew over to one of the cat beds I'd bought and settled into it, immediately falling asleep. He snored lightly.

"You're in for a ride," Bran said, following me as I headed for the door. "I remember Melda—she was a hoot. When my mother wasn't around, she used to perch on my head and let me walk around with her. I called her my dragon hat and both of us found that hilarious, for some reason."

We chatted about the herb garden as we headed outside. The sky was clear, although I could feel clouds on the outskirts, waiting to come in. But it wouldn't rain, I thought —not for a few days. The plants were reaching for the sun, drinking it in, and I was struck by the energy that buzzed through my land. Everything felt content—happy.

"What made you decide to become a farmer?" I asked.

"I don't consider myself a farmer. We tend to bees, and yes, I grow a large garden and we sell some of the produce at the market, but like you, my energy is with the earth. I just interact with it a different way I also connect to the air element, but not as strongly. I'm happiest when I'm shepherding things. We do keep pigs and chickens for meat, and a couple cows for milk as well. I like providing for my mother, and putting in an honest day's sweat."

Most witches had jobs other than relying on their magic, so it was no surprise to me that Bran worked a trade. But for some reason, he still struck me as an anachronism. Maybe that was *me*, though. I hadn't grown up in a big city, but Port Townsend was a little over three times the size of Starlight Hollow. Maybe I wasn't used to small-town life yet. It ran at a different pace.

Bran split off, heading to the area that would be my driveway, while I crossed to the workshop and unlocked the door. I had to start thinking of it as my *store*, though I wondered how many people would drive out here for magical supplies. I might have to rent a shop downtown if it didn't work out.

As I assembled spell kits—pulling herbs and candles, incense and crystals together in ways that would complement each other and adding an instruction sheet I'd written up and printed to each box—I paused to text a thank-you to May for the baked goods. Then I walked to the window and peeked outside, glancing at Bran. He'd taken his shirt off and was using stakes and twine to mark off the perimeters that would become the parking lot. The sweat glistened on his chest, and once again I found myself catching my breath.

"What's wrong with you?" I asked myself.

With Rian, I'd been sex-crazy. We'd been between the sheets at least once a day, every day. But since his death, I'd spent the past year ignoring every thought of men, sex, and dating. Now it felt like every man I saw was trying to awaken those old feelings in me. Well, not *every* man. Just two of them. Two men who happened to loathe each other. And two men who had both entered my life in very different ways.

I returned to the counter and sat on the tall stool, staring at the boxes laid out in front of me. My life had suddenly become a ball of yarn, twisted in knots that I'd never expected.

"What an apt metaphor," I whispered.

Finding Fancypants...meeting Bran...and then there was Faron, whom I had literally ran into, and who now was inexplicably tangled up in my life...

Unsure what to do, I continued to fashion the spell kits, trying to focus on the immediate task in front of me. But I finally had to move over to the computer I had installed in the workshop and turn on a streaming show to keep myself from falling deep into the whirlwind of my thoughts.

CHAPTER SEVENTEEN

AT TEN FORTY-FIVE, BRAN TAPPED ON THE DOOR OF THE workshop. I had managed to box up thirty spell kits for everything from protection to prosperity, and I was starting in on bagging an assortment of dried herbs into one-ounce packages when he interrupted.

I opened the door and there he stood, shirt in hand, skin glistening, hair loose and streaming around his shoulders. He'd draped a towel around his neck.

"Hey, I'm about to head home for the day. I thought I'd peek in and see how you're doing. Do you need anything else before I leave?" He glanced at the towering stack of spell kits. "It looks like you had a productive morning," he added with a smile.

"I did." Once I'd taken a few minutes to focus, I had slid into a rhythm and I was almost done with the work I wanted to get done for the day. Anything beyond this was gravy. I set the plastic bag down next to the pouch of rosemary.

"I can't think of much," I said after a minute.

Bran nodded. He started to withdraw, then stopped. "I'll be back Monday to work on the parking lot," he said, his hand on the door frame. "On the weekend, I spend mornings taking care of our books and bills, and planning out the week."

I had the feeling he wanted to say something else. "What is it?"

"So, what's your status with Faron?" he finally said.

I frowned. "I'm not sure I know what you mean by 'status.' "

"I mean, are you dating? Or are you..."

With a sudden flash of understanding, I realized what he meant. "Oh, that. Well, we've had one date. I enjoyed it but I said goodbye at the door, Bran, and he hasn't called. I'm not pining by the phone," I added, grinning. "I'm not nineteen."

"Good," he said, looking relieved. "Because I was wondering if you'd like to go on a picnic with me on Sunday? We can take Fancypants with us—I know a beautiful, shaded spot that's secluded."

I hesitated. "What about the murderer who's running around? Daisy says it's not safe to be out right now." While a picnic with Bran would be comfortable enough to manage, I'd seen the result of the serial killer's work.

His expression fell. "Crap, I didn't even think about that."

I didn't want to disappoint him, so I scrambled for an alternative. "What about if we have a picnic in your backyard? I love your flower gardens, and you do have a pond that's good for swimming in, from what I understand. I'll bring my bathing suit. May could join us."

In fact, from what I understood, Bran had installed a pump to keep the water circulating so that it didn't invite mosquitos, and the pond was as wide as a good-size house.

Bran flashed me a grateful look. "Sunday at four? Our backyard? You bring Fancypants—I'll take care of everything else." He glanced at the clock on my wall. "I need to get a move on for today. See you Sunday!"

He headed out, a spring in his step. I could feel the relief flooding off him, and I realized he'd been worried about my answer. I paused to mark the picnic down in my calendar on my phone, then went back to finishing up the herb packets. I wanted to be done for the day before I headed out to salt the bones and put the spirits to rest.

AT ONE FORTY-FIVE, I pulled up to Hatfield Cemetery. Daisy was already there, waiting. I parked next to her car and stepped out, gazing over the wide field in front of me. It wasn't meticulously groomed, yet it felt cared for and cherished. I closed my eyes and reached out, sensing a number of spirits wandering the graveyard. But none of them seemed inclined to bother me. They kept to themselves, and while I was curious why they hadn't passed through the Veil, I didn't feel any angst or desperation coming from the ghosts.

Daisy waved to me and stepped out of her car as I approached. "Hey there."

"Hi," I said, holding up a bag of spell supplies. "I brought everything I need."

I'd gathered graveyard dust mixed with black salt, then added a full five pounds of kosher salt and Exorcism oil. I was taking no chances. I wanted to put those two old broads to rest and make certain they were unable to return. I had texted Darla to meet me at her house afterward so we could destroy the material components of the spell. The possibility of recovering her husband from the clutches of the spirits had her scrambling to agree.

"So, what do you need to do?" Daisy asked as the gravediggers drove up in a hearse. They opened the back and began to unload two simple pine coffins. The city didn't spend more than they had to when it came to burying Jane

Does, which was fine with me given I detested the heavy caskets designed to defy time.

"I need to open the coffins and cover the bones with the salt mixture. The salt's enchanted, so it's simple enough, and it should break the connection of the skeletons to the items that were in that trunk. The skeletons were the anchors for the demons, and this will return them to the bones they're supposed to be."

Daisy frowned. "So, were the spirits not attached to the skeletons? As in, the spirits of the women who—I'm not sure what I'm asking here."

"I hear you. What you're asking is if the spirits haunting the attic were the spirits of the women who the skeletons belonged to. And to answer you: I don't think so. I believe that whoever set up this spell brought in two demonic spirits and tied them to the skeletons, creating a blend that created a new form of entity. The demons took on the persona of these two women. They essentially hijacked the women's spirits and tainted them with their own energy. The spell components—the knitting needles and hand mirror—opened the portal to invoke the demons."

As the gravediggers dug the graves, Daisy escorted me over to the coffins. She motioned to one of the gravediggers, who put down his shovel and came over to us.

"I need you to open these coffins," she said.

The man gave her an odd look, but did as she asked.

As the lids came off the coffins, the aged ivory of the bones glimmered starkly against the dark wood. Bare, stripped of the clothes we had found them in, I suddenly felt sorry for whomever the women had been. They had been disturbed in the grave—or never properly laid to rest—and used as a means to an end. It was possible they had been murdered, but we'd never know. And if they'd been murdered and never laid to rest, then their loved ones hadn't had a chance to say goodbye. If they'd already been dead and buried and stolen out of the grave, then their rest had been desecrated.

I approached the skeletons. I could still feel the energy surrounding them, but things were discombobulated and the demons weren't here in the cemetery. Bringing out my large box of the salt mixture, I stopped to say a quick prayer over the bones.

"We don't know who you were, or who you worshipped, but may this salting lay you to rest finally, breaking any attachments so you can move on. If your spirits can hear me, may you fly free and find your ancestors."

As I poured the salt over the bones, I could feel a stretching, as though the spirits were struggling to separate from the bones and the pull of the demons. The salt sizzled and popped as the grains touched the bones. I had no sooner poured all of the salt into the two coffins when there was a bright flash as smoke rose from the coffins and dissipated into the air.

"Half the battle done," I said, stepping back.

While Daisy motioned for the gravediggers to close up the coffins again, I texted Darla to ask if she had the knitting needles and other items.

I DO AND I'M BACK AT HOME. THINGS FEEL VERY WEIRD SO I'M SITTING OUTSIDE IN MY CAR. I TOLD GEORGIE TO WAIT AT THE HOTEL WITH THE KIDS. DO YOU REALLY THINK THIS WILL WORK?

I HOPE SO. I FINISHED SALTING THE BONES AND IT HAD A NOTICEABLE EFFECT. I'LL BE THERE IN TEN MINUTES AND HOPEFULLY WE'LL PUT AN END TO THIS.

I glanced up at Daisy. "I'm headed over to Darla's to finish this exorcism. Thank you. You don't know what a help this has been." I pointed to the coffins. The gravediggers had affixed the lids again, and now they were back to digging. "Tell me, will you put up markers?"

"We can't afford much, but we'll erect stones to mark their graves," Daisy said.

"Let me know when they're up, and I'll bring out some flowers." It was the least I could do. Somebody needed to remember the nameless, and I was willing to do that.

I ARRIVED at Darla's shortly afterward. She was waiting for me—as she had said—in her car. A box sat on the hood and as I hopped out of my car and approached her, she pointed to it.

"There are the things. I didn't have the courage to go back inside by myself." She looked harried and tired, with dark circles under her eyes. She looked like she hadn't had any sleep since Tuesday night and here it was Friday.

"I'm glad you didn't. When I salted the bones, it was bound to stir things up. I'll take those items into the basement and destroy them and that should be it." I patted her on the shoulder. "Whatever you do, don't come in."

"What if you're in trouble?" she asked.

"I'll be fine," I said, not sure if I believed it. But I picked up the box of items and took the key Darla gave me and headed into the house.

THE HOUSE FELT different than when I'd last been there. The spirits had been up in arms, intent on chasing us out. Now, though they were still here, the energy was tilt-a-whirl crazy, a runaway force spinning without someone to slow it down.

I knew what had happened to cause the shift.

When I had salted the bones, it had broken the demons

away from their anchors, and freed the spirits they had taken over. The demons were still trapped within the house because the items used to keep them there were still whole and in my possession. I could feel them spinning around me in a crazed circle. But they couldn't use the anchors to direct their attacks. Nothing happened when I entered the house, but they knew I was here, and probably knew that I was about ready to dispel them.

I headed for the basement.

"I can handle this," I whispered to myself as I descended the stairs, cautiously steadying myself against the wall.

The bare light bulb swayed on its own as I made my way through the stacks of boxes, nerves alight and ready for a confrontation. I was in danger and I knew it. I pulled out my phone and set it on the box next to the trunk.

After placing all the items in the trunk, I pulled out a bottle of water. It had occurred to me that since metal knitting needles couldn't burn and neither could a piece of obsidian, fire wouldn't take care of everything. But fire and water together were a potent mix.

I began by opening the jar of hellebore and scattering it in the trunk. Next, I unraveled the partly knitted potholder and coiled the yarn on top of the hellebore. Then, using a lighter, I lit on fire the paper with the incantation written on it and held it over the herbs and yarn until it was flickering brightly as the flames ate away at the page.

Before the flames could reach my fingers, I dropped the burning paper onto the pile, but the yarn didn't take and the herbs were so dusty that they just sputtered.

"Well, at least the paper burned," I said. I brought out a bottle of blessed moon water that I had made and poured it into the trunk, saturating everything. Then I picked up the obsidian and, standing back, I threw it into the trunk as hard as I could. It splintered into a hundred shards.

The moment the obsidian shattered, the energy in the basement began to shake. Boxes flew off the stacks, shooting across the room. I yelped, ducking as one nearly hit me in the head. The next moment, I smelled something burning and glanced back at the trunk. Smoke and flames were billowing out of it, flickering up to set on fire some of the papers in a nearby box.

What the fuck? The flame had refused to take when I tried to burn the herbs and yarn! Where had they come from?

Then common sense took over and I grabbed my phone, dialing Darla. "Call the fire department immediately. Fire in the basement."

"Get out of there now! I'll call 911." She hung up.

I looked around to see that the fire was already spreading through the boxes of junk and old magazines that filled the basement, jumping from box to box like a wildfire crowning the top of the trees. A thick, oily smoke was beginning to spread, filling the air. I coughed, trying to see through the haze. I stumbled over a box and realized that I had gotten turned around and I was going the wrong way.

How do I get out? I was beginning to panic. I couldn't see the floor and now the flames surrounded me. I tried to think of a spell to quench them, but the fear crowding my mind was so strong that it pushed everything away.

"Ouch!"

I jumped as a tongue of flame licked against my arm. Pulling to the side, I realized that I was next to the shelves holding the old jars of canned food. The narrow aisle between the stacks of junk and the shelves was now covered with burning debris, preventing my escape.

Maybe I could climb the shelves and pull myself up onto the staircase. Dizzy from the smoke, I put my foot on the second shelf and reached up, catching hold of one of the upper shelves. Neither felt very sturdy and the wood wobbled like it could give at any minute.

I was most of the way up and had managed to catch hold of the side of the step above when the wood beneath my foot broke and I found myself hanging by one hand. Desperate, I jostled, trying to swing my feet up to the next shelf. But there was another splintering sound and the next moment, I fell onto the floor, flat on my back. Frustrated and now terrified, I let out a scream. I didn't want to die like this—not by fire.

The next moment, Fancypants appeared by my side. Startled, I sat up.

"You have to get out of here—you'll get hurt," I exclaimed.

"You're in danger. I'm sorry I wasn't here earlier," Fancypants said. "I had to get help."

"What—help?" I pressed back against the shelves, my head beginning to cloud. My lungs were burning, and I was having trouble keeping my eyes open.

Fancypants said nothing, but the next moment, I heard a hissing all around me. The flames near me sizzled, and it occurred to me that I was getting wet. But before I could figure out what was happening, the world began to spin.

"I can't bre—" I started to say, but the room faded in and out and everything went black.

CHAPTER EIGHTEEN

"ELPHYRA? ELPHYRA, SAY SOMETHING!"

The voice slicing through the fog sounded familiar. I tried to open my eyes, but they felt so glued together that I could barely peek through them. My throat was raw and I had a splitting headache. My lungs were so tight that I might as well be wearing a waist-constricting corset.

"What happened?" I asked, prying my eyes open. I winced as the early evening sunlight hit my face.

"Are you all right?" Bran was kneeling beside me. He was disheveled, his hair hanging loose, his shirt covered with soot. He had a bright red mark on his arm that looked like a burn.

"I don't know...I think so, though my throat feels like it's on fire." I looked into Bran's eyes as he knelt beside me. "How did you know— Fancypants! Where's Fancypants?"

"Fancypants's fine. He came to get me and told me that you were in life-threatening danger. I texted Daisy and she said you'd been headed for Darla's house. She gave me the address and said a call had just come in that the house was on fire. Fancypants vanished and I guess he showed up here, traveling via Sescernaht. He stayed by your side until I managed to get here and carry you out of the basement." Bran reached down and stroked my hair back. "I want the doctor to examine you."

I struggled to say I was okay, but was overcome by a coughing fit. But inside, all I could think of was that Fancypants had saved my life. Fancypants and Bran. When I could talk again, I asked, "How long was it before the firefighters arrived?"

"They arrived about five minutes after I did. They're still fighting the fire. If I hadn't been able to pull you out of the basement when I did..."

"I would have died," I said. "How did Fancypants know I was in danger?"

I stopped. *The bond.* Fancypants had felt my fear and panic through our bond. As I sat there, propped up and leaning against Bran, it dawned on me that Rian was right. I really *wasn't* alone anymore. Fancypants was there for me, no matter what.

"Where is he?" I asked, looking around.

"He went back to your house once he knew you were going to be all right." Bran slid his arm around my shoulders. "Hold still. I'm going to carry you over to the EMTs. They're experienced in treating those in the Otherkin community."

"I can walk—" I started to say, but Bran shook his head.

"You twisted your ankle, I think. Don't you notice the pain?"

I glanced down at my foot and started to turn my ankle. A sharp pain sliced through me. "Damn it! What the hell...Oh, that's right. I was trying to climb the shelves to get to the stairs when they broke and I fell." I frowned. "How did you know that I hurt my ankle?"

"When I found you, it was turned in a most disturbing way." Bran shifted me in his arms.

He smelled like smoke and dirt and sweat, but right now

he might as well have smelled like a cinnamon roll on steroids. He had saved me, and all I could think of was that I owed him my life and my gratitude.

I leaned against his shoulder, tired and sore. Everything hurt now that I was conscious. I glanced back at the house, which was still on fire. Darla was standing by her car, a horrified look on her face. She saw Bran carrying me over to the medic unit and hurried over.

"How are you? I was so afraid you weren't going to make it out." She fussed over me, but stood back when the paramedics took me from Bran and sat me down.

After they examined my lungs, a few burns that I hadn't managed to escape, and my ankle—which they didn't know if it was fractured or sprained—they declared I needed to go to the hospital. Without further ado, the medics loaded me into the ambulance and took off.

THE NURSE ADJUSTED the hospital bed so I was reclining at a slight angle but still high enough to help me with the cough that the smoke had triggered. Bran and May were there, waiting with me, as the doctor came in. Her name was Patricia Hagg, and she was blunt but polite.

"Well, we have the results of your X-rays. You don't have a fracture, but I'm still going to put you in a walking cast for a month. You'll heal faster that way." She checked her clipboard, aka my file. "Your lungs took a beating. I'm going to prescribe an inhaler for you, again for a month. It should help minimize the damage. As far as the burns go, we'll dress them, but none are serious. Consider yourself one lucky woman. Now, you're Otherkin?"

I nodded. "I'm magic-born."

"Then I'll make sure the meds and the pain med I'm going to prescribe you aren't contraindicated."

"How soon till you can release me?"

"As soon as we put you in that cast and the nurse dresses your burns." She paused. "Do you have any questions about your treatment?"

I shook my head. "No, thanks. If I forget, I can call."

As she left, I glanced over at May and Bran. For the first time in a year, I felt safe. At least, safe for the moment. I didn't know how to thank them, but I was grateful they had come into my life, and maybe they could teach me how to step out of the self-imposed prison I had created for myself.

THAT NIGHT, once I was home with May ensconced in the guest room, I leaned against the headboard, my foot raised on several pillows. I was about to ask for help out to the recliner when Fancypants appeared on the bed next to me.

"I'm so glad you're okay," he said.

"Listen—I owe you a huge debt. I wouldn't be alive if it weren't for you and for Bran." I paused, closing my eyes. I could feel Fancypants's trill of satisfaction, his joy in talking to me. I could feel the bond between us on a tangible level, and my heart welled up. "I'm so glad you found me," I whispered, stretching out my hand.

Fancypants stepped on my palm. He held onto my thumb, rubbing his cheek against it. "You're my person. I'm your dragonette."

I curled up under the covers and instantly fell asleep.

TWO WEEKS LATER...

Bree and I were sitting outside on the patio. I stretched out my foot. "I can hardly wait to get rid of this cast. I'm so tired of it."

"How long do you have left?"

"Two more weeks." I paused, then asked, "Have you heard from Darla lately?"

"Yeah, she and Kevin are back together and he's back to normal. They sold the land and the remains of the house and they're looking to move out of town. I don't think Starlight Hollow has much to offer them. At least he's back to being a loving husband and father. She says next house, they're buying a new build and doing research on the land first." Bree stared at the herb garden. "What about your mother?"

"She's coming down this weekend. I finally caved and said all right. She'll stay for a week to help me out until I get this cast off. I'm healing up faster than expected, so just one week left."

"Good, I'd like to see her," Bree said.

"I still haven't told her my great-grandma's coming in another two weeks. I'll wait till she gets here. They never got along very well, so I doubt my mother will want to stick around for that visit."

"Yeah, I remember some of your mother's stories about her." Bree sighed. "There was another murder last night. That's four."

"I heard. I was hoping that the killer had moved on. It's almost scarier that he let time go by between Jimithy's murder and this one. That says to me that he's calculating, not an opportunist."

The murders had clouded Starlight Hollow's charm and everybody in town seemed guarded. During summer, the bicyclists and hikers and joggers should be out in full force, but the streets were empty at night and everyone seemed in a hurry to get home.

"Daisy still thinks Elroy's trouble, but he has an airtight alibi for the third, so she's finally looking elsewhere. But if he's not the murderer, that means another wolf shifter is. Unless Jimithy was wrong."

"Do you think Jimithy was wrong?" Bree asked.

I shook my head. "No, I don't. By the way, May broke the bonds between the Butcher and me a couple days ago. It was odd and I was kind of freaked out, but it's done. He probably felt it, but now he can't find me through them."

"That's one bright spot. As far as the murderer goes, there's not much we can do about it right now. Take precautions and let the sheriff do her job." Bree helped me up and we headed over toward the new parking lot that Bran had finished. It would hold eight cars, and the signs he had made for me were gorgeous. Elegant and refined, the woodcarving on them was brilliant. "So, are you and Bran dating?"

"Maybe. I don't know. I'm maybe kind of dating Faron, too. I like both of them, and yet...am I ready to date *anyone* yet?" I sighed. "I'm trying to keep things casual."

"You want my opinion?" Bree asked as we headed back to the house. It was nearing dinner time.

"Do I have a choice or are you going to give it to me regardless of what I say?"

"The latter," she said. "I think you should take it slow, enjoy the company of both, and then decide later if and when it becomes an issue."

"I'm good with that." I glanced at the sky. It was nearly five. "Okay, what say you and I and Fancypants toss the pizzas I bought into the oven and watch a marathon of *Terafin House*?"

Terafin House was the latest period piece—half romance, half drama, and all highly romanticized fantasy. And given all the grim things in my life lately, it was exactly what the doctor ordered. As we laughed and went inside, locking the night away, I stared out the window for a moment before shutting the curtains. With a murderer on the prowl, it seemed the cautious move to make.

Fancypants joined us as we curled up on the sofa with ice cream. The pizzas were baking, giving off a delicious tomato-yeasty aroma, and everything inside felt comfortable and cozy. But I could feel that, just outside the window, out in the world, events were brewing. I could feel them as certain as I could feel my heart beat. And whatever was on the way felt foreign and strange...with a glimmer of danger hiding behind it.

FOR MORE OF **the Starlight Hollow Series**, you can preorder Elphyra's second book. Together with her red drag-onette, Fancypants, she both protects *and* heats up the town in every sense of the word. Preorder the second book, **Starlight Dreams**, now!

For more of the Moonshadow Bay Series: January Jaxson returns to the quirky town of Moonshadow Bay after her husband dumps her and steals their business, and within days she's working for Conjure Ink, a paranormal investigations agency, and exploring the potential of her hot new neighbor. Ten books (including this one) are currently available. You can preorder **Dreamer's Web** now! If you haven't read the other books in this series, begin with **Starlight Web**.

For all the rest of my current and finished series, check out my State of the Series page, and you can also check the Bibliography the end of this book, or check out my website at **Galenorn.com** and be sure and sign up for my **newsletter** to receive news about all my new releases. Also, you're welcome to join my YouTube Channel community.

QUALITY CONTROL: This work has been professionally edited and proofread. If you encounter any typos or formatting issues ONLY, please contact me through my **website** so they may be corrected. Otherwise, know that this book is in my style and voice and editorial suggestions will not be entertained. Thank you.

PLAYLIST

I often write to music, and STARLIGHT HOLLOW was no exception. Here's the playlist I used for this book. You'll notice a distinct difference from most of my playlists, but this is what the mood of the book wanted.

- **Alice in Chains:** Man in the Box
- **Android Lust:** Here and Now
- **The Animals:** Story of Bo Diddley; Bury My Body
- **The Asteroids Galaxy Tour:** The Sun Ain't Shining No More; Heart Attack; The Golden Age; Around the Bend; Major
- **Awolnation:** Sail
- **Beats Antique:** Runaway; Vardo; Tabla Toy
- **Beck:** Emergency Exit; Farewell Ride
- **The Bravery:** Believe
- **Brent Lewis:** Beyond Midnight; Joy
- **Broken Bells:** The Ghost Inside
- **Celtic Woman:** The Butterfly
- **Circle of Women:** Mother of Darkness
- **Clannad:** Banba Óir; I See Red

- **Cream:** Strange Brew
- **Creedence Clearwater Revival:** Born on the Bayou
- **Crosby, Stills, & Nash:** Guinnevere
- **David Bowie:** Without You; China Girl
- **David & Steve Gordon:** Shaman's Drum Dance; Eagle's Rhythm Gift
- **Dead Can Dance:** Yulunga; The Ubiquitous Mr. Lovegrove; Indus
- **Deuter:** Petite Fleur
- **Dizzi:** Dizzi Jig; Dance of the Unicorns
- **DJ Shah:** Mellomaniac
- **Donovan:** Sunshine Superman; Season of the Witch
- **Dragon Ritual Drummers:** Black Queen; The Fall
- **Eastern Sun:** Beautiful Being
- **Enya:** Orinoco Flow
- **Everlast:** Ends; Black Jesus
- **Faun:** Rad; Sieben
- **Finger Eleven:** Paralyzer
- **Fleetwood Mac:** The Chain
- **Flight of the Hawk:** Bones
- **Foster the People:** Pumped Up Kicks
- **Gabrielle Roth:** The Calling; Raven; Cloud Mountain; Rest Your Tears Here; Zone Unknown; Avenue A
- **Godsmack:** Voodoo
- **Gorillaz:** Rockit; Stylo; Hongkongaton; Clint Eastwood; Dare; Demon Days
- **Halsey:** Castle
- **Hedningarna:** Grodan/Widergrenen; Räven; Tullí; Ukkonen; Juopolle Joutunut; Gorrlaus
- **Imagine Dragons:** Natural

- **J. Rokka:** Marine Migration
- **Jethro Tull:** Jack-A-Lynn; Rhythm in Gold; Overhang; Witch's Promise; No Lullaby; Sweet Dream; Old Ghosts; Dun Ringill
- **John Fogerty:** Old Man Down the Road
- **Kevin Morby:** Beautiful Strangers
- **Loreena McKennitt:** The Mummer's Dance; The Mystic's Dream; All Souls Night
- **Low:** Plastic Cup; Witches; Half Light
- **Marconi Union:** First Light; Alone Together; Flying; Always Numb; On Reflection; Broken Colours; Weightless
- **Meditative Mind:** Hang Drum + Tabla Music for Yoga; Hang Drum + Water Drums
- **Motherdrum:** Big Stomp
- **The Notwist:** Hands on Us
- **Orgy:** Blue Monday; Social Enemies
- **Pati Yang:** All That Is Thirst
- **Rob Zombie:** Living Dead Girl; Dragula
- **Rue du Soleil:** We Can Fly; Le Francaise; Wake Up Brother; Blues Du Soleil
- **Saliva:** Ladies and Gentlemen
- **Seether:** Remedy
- **Seth Glier:** The Next Right Thing
- **SJ Tucker:** Hymn to Herne
- **Sharon Knight:** Ravage Ruins; Berrywood Grove; Star of the Sea; Siren Moon; Song of the Sea
- **Shriekback:** This Big Hush; Underwaterboys; The King in the Tree
- **Spiral Dance:** Boys of Bedlam; Burning Times; Rise Up
- **St. Vincent:** Pay Your Way In Pain
- **Steeleye Span:** The Fox

- **Strawberry Alarm Clock:** Incense and Peppermint
- **Tamaryn:** While You're Sleeping, I'm Dreaming; Violet's in a Pool
- **Toadies:** Possum Kingdom
- **Tom Petty:** Mary Jane's Last Dance
- **Trills:** Speak Loud
- **Tuatha Dea:** Tuatha De Danaan; The Hum and the Shiver; Wisp of a Thing (Part 1); Long Black Curl
- **Wendy Rule:** Let the Wind Blow; The Circle Song
- **White Zombie:** More Human than Human
- **Zayde Wolf:** Gladiator
- **Zero 7:** In the Waiting Line

BIOGRAPHY

New York Times, *Publishers Weekly*, and *USA Today* bestselling author Yasmine Galenorn writes urban fantasy and para-normal romance, and is the author of over one hundred books, including the Wild Hunt Series, the Fury Unbound Series, the Bewitching Bedlam Series, the Indigo Court Series, and the Otherworld Series, among others. She's also written nonfiction metaphysical books. She is the 2011 Career Achievement Award Winner in Urban Fantasy, given by RT Magazine. Yasmine has been in the Craft since 1980, is a shamanic witch and High Priestess. She describes her life as a blend of teacups and tattoos. She lives in Kirkland, WA, with her husband Samwise and their cats. Yasmine can be reached via her website at **Galenorn.com**. You can find all her links at her **LinkTree**.

Indie Releases Currently Available:

Moonshadow Bay Series:
    Starlight Web
    Midnight Web

Conjure Web
Harvest Web
Shadow Web
Weaver's Web
Crystal Web
Witch's Web
Cursed Web
Solstice Web
Dreamer's Web

Night Queen Series:
    Tattered Thorns
    Shattered Spells
    Fractured Flowers

Starlight Hollow Series:
    Starlight Hollow
    Starlight Dreams

Magic Happens Series:
    Shadow Magic
    Charmed to Death

Hedge Dragon Series:
    The Poisoned Forest
    The Tangled Sky

The Wild Hunt Series:
    The Silver Stag
    Oak & Thorns
    Iron Bones
    A Shadow of Crows
    The Hallowed Hunt
    The Silver Mist

Witching Hour
Witching Bones
A Sacred Magic
The Eternal Return
Sun Broken
Witching Moon
Autumn's Bane
Witching Time
Hunter's Moon
Witching Fire
Veil of Stars
Antlered Crown

Lily Bound Series
    Soul Jacker

Chintz 'n China Series:
    Ghost of a Chance
    Legend of the Jade Dragon
    Murder Under a Mystic Moon
    A Harvest of Bones
    One Hex of a Wedding
    Holiday Spirits
    Well of Secrets
    Chintz 'n China Books, 1 – 3: Ghost of a Chance, Legend of the Jade Dragon, Murder Under A Mystic Moon
    Chintz 'n China Books, 4-6: A Harvest of Bones, One Hex of a Wedding, Holiday Spirits

Whisper Hollow Series:
    Autumn Thorns
    Shadow Silence
    The Phantom Queen

Bewitching Bedlam Series:
    Bewitching Bedlam
    Maudlin's Mayhem
    Siren's Song
    Witches Wild
    Casting Curses
    Demon's Delight
    Bedlam Calling: A Bewitching Bedlam Anthology
    Wish Factor (a prequel short story)
    Blood Music (a prequel novella)
    Blood Vengeance (a Bewitching Bedlam novella)
    Tiger Tails (a Bewitching Bedlam novella)

Fury Unbound Series:
    Fury Rising
    Fury's Magic
    Fury Awakened
    Fury Calling
    Fury's Mantle

Indigo Court Series:
    Night Myst
    Night Veil
    Night Seeker
    Night Vision
    Night's End
    Night Shivers
    Indigo Court Books, 1-3: Night Myst, Night Veil, Night Seeker (Boxed Set)
    Indigo Court Books, 4-6: Night Vision, Night's End, Night Shivers (Boxed Set)

Otherworld Series:
    Moon Shimmers

Harvest Song
Blood Bonds
Otherworld Tales: Volume 1
Otherworld Tales: Volume 2
For the rest of the Otherworld Series, see website at
Galenorn.com.

Bath and Body Series (originally under the name India Ink):
    Scent to Her Grave
    A Blush With Death
    Glossed and Found

Misc. Short Stories/Anthologies:
    The Longest Night (A Pagan Romance Novella)

Magickal Nonfiction: A Witch's Guide Series.
    Embracing the Moon
    Tarot Journeys
    Totem Magick

Printed in Great Britain
by Amazon